ALSO BY LYNDA MULLALY HUNT

One for the Murphys

Lynda Mullaly Hunt

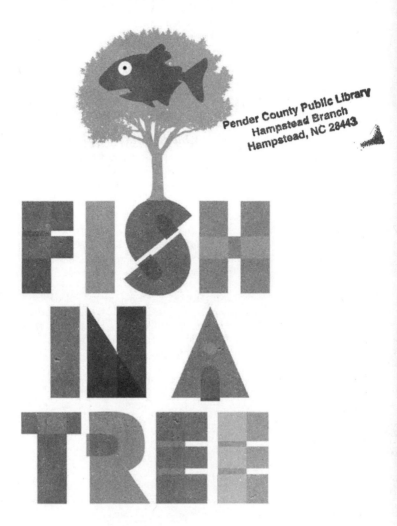

Nancy Paulsen Books ◉ An Imprint of Penguin Group (USA)

NANCY PAULSEN BOOKS
Published by the Penguin Group
Penguin Group (USA) LLC
375 Hudson Street, New York, NY 10014

USA | Canada | UK | Ireland | Australia
New Zealand | India | South Africa | China
penguin.com
A Penguin Random House Company

Library of Congress Cataloging-in-Publication Data is available upon request.

Printed in the United States of America.
ISBN 978-0-399-16259-6
17 19 20 18 16

Design by Ryan Thomann. Text set in Berling.
Fish and tree silhouettes used under license from Shutterstock.com.
Title lettering by Kristin Logsdon.

For teachers . . .
who see the child before the student,
who remind us that we all have
special gifts to offer the world,
who foster the importance of standing out
rather than fitting in.

And for kids . . .
who find their grit to conquer life's challenges—
no matter what those challenges may be.

You are heroes.

This book is for you.

Contents

CHAPTER 1

In Trouble Again

It's always there. Like the ground underneath my feet.

"Well, Ally? Are you going to write or aren't you?" Mrs. Hall asks.

If my teacher were mean it would be easier.

"C'mon," she says. "I know you can do it."

"What if I told you that I was going to climb a tree using only my teeth? Would you say I could *do it* then?"

Oliver laughs, throwing himself on his desk like it's a fumbled football.

Shay groans. "Ally, why can't you just act normal for once?"

Near her, Albert, a bulky kid who's worn the same

thing every day—a dark T-shirt that reads *Flint*—sits up straight. Like he's waiting for a firecracker to go off.

Mrs. Hall sighs. "C'mon, now. I'm only asking for one page describing yourself."

I can't think of anything worse than having to describe myself. I'd rather write about something more positive. Like throwing up at your own birthday party.

"It's important," she says. "It's so your new teacher can get to know you."

I know that, and it's exactly why I don't want to do it. Teachers are like the machines that take quarters for bouncy balls. You know what you're going to get. Yet, you don't know, too.

"And," she says, "all that doodling of yours, Ally. If you weren't drawing all the time, your work might be done. Please put it away."

Embarrassed, I slide my drawings underneath my blank writing assignment. I've been drawing pictures of myself being shot out of a cannon. It would be easier than school. Less painful.

"C'mon," she says, moving my lined paper toward me. "Just do your best."

Seven schools in seven years and they're all the same. Whenever I do my best, they tell me I don't try hard enough. Too messy. Careless spelling. Annoyed that the same word is spelled different ways on the same page. And the headaches. I always get headaches from looking at the brightness of dark letters on white pages for too long.

Mrs. Hall clears her throat.

The rest of the class is getting tired of me again. Chairs slide. Loud sighs. Maybe they think I can't hear their words: *Freak. Dumb. Loser.*

I wish she'd just go hang by Albert, the walking Google page who'd get a better grade than me if he just blew his nose into the paper.

The back of my neck heats up.

I don't get it. She always lets me slide. It must be because these are for the new teacher and she can't have one missing.

I stare at her big stomach. "So, did you decide what you're going to name the baby?" I ask. Last week we got her talking about baby names for a full half hour of social studies.

"C'mon, Ally. No more stalling."

I don't answer.

"I mean it," she says, and I know she does.

I watch a mind movie of her taking a stick and drawing a line in the dirt between us under a bright blue sky. She's dressed as a sheriff and I'm wearing black-and-white prisoner stripes. My mind does this all the time—shows me these movies that seem so real that they carry me away inside of them. They are a relief from my real life.

I steel up inside, willing myself to do something I don't really want to do. To escape this teacher who's holding on and won't let go.

I pick up my pencil and her body relaxes, probably relieved that I've given in.

But, instead, knowing she loves clean desks and things just so, I grip my pencil with a hard fist. And scribble all over my desk.

"*Ally!*" She steps forward quick. "Why would you *do* that?"

The circular scribbles are big on top and small on the bottom. It looks like a tornado and I wonder if I meant to draw a picture of my insides. I look back up at her. "It was there when I sat down."

The laughter starts—but they're not laughing because they think I'm funny.

"I can tell that you're upset, Ally," Mrs. Hall says.

I am not hiding that as well as I need to.

"She's such a freak," Shay says in one of those loud whispers that everyone is meant to hear.

Oliver is drumming on his desk now.

I fold my arms and stare up at her.

"That's *it*," Mrs. Hall finally says. "To the office. *Now.*"

I wanted this but now I am having second thoughts.

"*Ally.*"

"Huh?"

Everyone laughs again. She puts up her hand. "Anyone else who makes a sound gives up their recess." The room is quiet.

"Ally. I *said* to the office."

I can't go see our principal, Mrs. Silver, again. I go to the office so much, I wonder when they'll hang up a banner that says WELCOME, ALLY NICKERSON!

"I'm sorry," I say, actually meaning it. "I'll do it. I promise."

She sighs. "Okay, Ally, but if that pencil stops moving, you're *going.*"

She moves me to the reading table next to a Thanksgiving bulletin board about being grateful. Meanwhile, she sprays my desk with cleaner. Glancing at me like she'd like to spray *me* with cleaner. Scrub off the dumb.

I squint a bit, hoping the lights will hurt my head less. And then I try to hold my pencil the way I'm supposed to instead of the weird way my hand wants to.

I write with one hand and shield my paper with the other. I know I better keep the pencil moving, so I write the word "Why?" over and over from the top of the page to the very bottom.

One, because I know how to spell it right and two, because I'm hoping someone will finally give me an answer.

CHAPTER 2

Yellow Card

For Mrs. Hall's baby shower, Jessica shows up with such a big bunch of flowers from her father's florist shop that you'd swear she ripped a bush out of the ground and wrapped the bottom in foil.

Whatever. I don't care. I found a bright card with yellow roses at the store. And a picture of flowers won't dry up in a week. I feel like it's my way of saying I'm sorry for being such a pain all the time.

Max gives his present to Mrs. Hall. He leans back in his chair with his hands clasped behind his head as she opens it. He's given her diapers. I think he hoped to get a reaction from her and seems disappointed when she's happy.

Max likes attention. He also likes parties. Just about

every day, he asks Mrs. Hall for a party, and today, he's finally getting one.

When Mrs. Hall slides my card out of the envelope, she doesn't read it out loud like all the others. She hesitates, and I know that she must really love it. And I feel proud, which isn't something I feel very much.

Mrs. Silver leans over to look. I figure I might finally get a compliment for once, but instead, her eyebrows bunch up and she motions me toward the door.

Shay has gotten up to look. She laughs and says, "The world gets dumber every time Ally Nickerson speaks."

"Shay. *Sit* down," Mrs. Hall says, but it's too late. You can't make people unhear something. I should be used to this, but it still takes a piece out of me every time.

As Shay and Jessica laugh, I remember how we dressed up as our favorite book characters for Halloween last week. I came as Alice in Wonderland, from the book my grandpa read to me a ton of times. Shay and her shadow, Jessica, called me Alice in Blunderland all day.

Keisha steps up to Shay and says, "Why don't you mind your own business for once?"

I like Keisha. She isn't afraid. And I'm afraid of so much.

Shay turns, looking like she's ready to swat a fly. "Like it's *your* business?" she asks her.

"That's right. It's *not* my business, but it's as much yours . . . as it is mine," Keisha replies.

Shay lets out a small gasp. "*Stop* talking to me."

"*Stop* being mean," Keisha replies, leaning forward.

Max folds his arms and leans forward across his desk. "*Yes*. There's going to be a fight," he says.

"There's *isn't* going to be a *fight*," Mrs. Hall says.

Suki is holding one of her small wooden blocks. She has a collection of them that she keeps in a box and I've seen her take one out when she gets nervous. She's nervous now.

Shay glares at Keisha. Keisha is new this year and I'm surprised she's said something.

Everyone is all riled up and I don't even know how this all happened.

While Mrs. Hall tells them both to cool off and points out to Max that it's foolish to root for a fight, Mrs. Silver waves me toward the door. What the heck is going on?

Once we're out in the hallway, I can tell by Mrs. Silver's face that it's going to be another one of those times when I'll have to say I'm sorry or explain why I've done something. The thing is, I have no idea why I'm even in trouble this time.

I stuff my hands in my pockets to keep them from doing something I'll regret. I wish I could put my mouth in there, too.

"I just don't get it, Ally," she says. "You've done other

things that have been inappropriate, but this is just . . . well . . . *different*. It's not like you."

It figures; I do something *nice* and she says it isn't like me. And I can't understand how buying a card is bad.

"Ally," Mrs. Silver says. "If you're looking for attention, this isn't the way to do it."

She has that wrong. I need attention like a fish needs a snorkel.

The door swings all the way open, hitting the lockers, and Oliver springs from the room. "Ally," he says. "I think you gave her that card to tell her you're sorry she has to leave us to go have some dumb baby. She's probably really sad. I feel sorry for her, too."

What is he *talking* about?

"Oliver?" Mrs. Silver asks. "Is there a reason you're out here?"

"Yeah! I was going to . . . um . . . I was . . . going to go to the boys' room. Yeah. That's it." And off he runs.

"Can I just go now?" I blurt out, feeling like the job of just standing here is something I can't do for another second.

She shakes her head a bit as she speaks. "I just don't get it. Why in the *world* would you give a pregnant woman a sympathy card?"

Sympathy card? I think. And I think some more. And

then I remember. My mom sends those to people when someone they love dies. My stomach churns, wondering what Mrs. Hall must have thought.

"You do know what a sympathy card *is*, Ally, don't you?"

I should deny that I know, but I nod because I don't want to have to hear Mrs. Silver explain it. And besides, she'll think I'm even dumber than I am. If that's possible.

"Then why would you do such a thing?"

I stand tall, but everything inside shrinks. The thing is, I feel real bad. I mean, I felt terrible when the neighbor's dog died, never mind if a baby had died. I just didn't know it was a sad card like that. All I could see were beautiful yellow flowers. And all I could imagine was how happy I was going to make her.

But there are piles of reasons I can't tell the absolute truth.

Not to her.

Not to anyone.

No matter how many times I have prayed and worked and hoped, reading for me is still like trying to make sense of a can of alphabet soup that's been dumped on a plate. I just don't know how other people do it.

CHAPTER 3

Never up to Me

Leaning against the wall in the hallway, I stay quiet.
Some little kids walk by, reminding me that I'm in sixth grade—the highest grade in this school. But I feel like a baby.

"Ally? Do you have anything to say?" Mrs. Silver asks.

I'm afraid to open my mouth because sometimes things just come out that get me in more trouble.

Finally, she suggests we go to her office.

I sit in the principal's office staring out the window, silent. I wonder what it would be like to be able to relax at school and not have to worry every second of every minute.

I wish I had my Sketchbook of Impossible Things. It's

the only thing that makes me feel like I'm not a waste of space. I like to watch the pictures in my head become real in my book. My recent favorite is a snowman that works in a furnace factory. And then I decide that the craziest, strangest, most unbelievable thing I could ever draw is me doing something right.

Mrs. Silver's sigh brings me back to reality. "Between last year and this year, you've been here for less than five months, Ally, and you've been to visit me far too much. You need to make some changes," she says.

I sit silent.

"It's up to you."

It's not up to me. It's *never* been up to me.

Mrs. Silver's talking is like background noise. Like the radio in the car.

I don't have any words to explain. It was a mistake. And I'm ashamed and I don't feel like sharing that with her.

She takes a breath. "Did you think it would be funny?"

I shake my head.

"Did you want to hurt her?"

I look up quick. "No! I wouldn't hurt her. I just . . ."

And I wonder what I've wondered before. Should I just tell her? It's like my chair is over a trapdoor and there is a button to drop myself. I want to, but I'm afraid. I look up at her. Looking at me all disappointed. Again. And I think that there's no use. They already think I'm a pain, so why add *dumb* to their list? It's not like they can help, anyway. How can you cure dumb?

And so I look out the window again. Remind my mouth to keep shut.

I've learned from the seven different schools I've been to that it's better to stay quiet. Never argue unless I really have to.

I realize that both of my hands have curled into tight fists and Mrs. Silver is looking at them.

She sits down in the chair next to me. "Ally, sometimes it seems that you just *want* to get into trouble." She leans forward a bit. "*Do* you?"

I shake my head.

"C'mon, Ally. Tell me what's going on. Let me help you."

I look at her quick and then away. I mumble, "*No one can help me.*"

"That's not true. Will you let me try?" She points at a poster on the wall. "Can you read that for me, please?" she says. "Out loud."

The poster shows two hands reaching for each other.

Great. Probably some sappy saying about friends or sticking together or whatever. I don't even have any friends.

"C'mon, Ally. Read it for me, please."

The letters on the poster look like black beetles marching across the wall. I could probably figure most of them out, but I'd need a lot of time. And when I'm nervous, forget it. My brain goes blank like an Etch A Sketch turned upside down and shaken. Gray and empty.

"Well, what does it say?" she asks again.

"I don't need to read it to you. I get it," I say, trying to bluff. Staring her dead in the eyes. "Believe me. I know all about it already."

"I don't know about that, kiddo. I think you might need to work on it a bit."

Now I wish I knew what the poster said. I don't look at it, though. Then she'll want to talk about it more.

The bell rings.

Mrs. Silver rakes her hair with her fingers. "Ally. I don't know if you thought the card would be funny or you are upset that Mrs. Hall's leaving or what. But it feels like you've crossed a line this time."

I imagine myself crossing the finish line. My body breaking the bright red ribbon. The crowd cheering as confetti spins through the air. But I know this is not what she means.

"As of Monday, your new teacher will be Mr. Daniels. Let's try to avoid any negative consequences, okay?"

I think about how me avoiding *consequences* would be like the rain avoiding the sky.

She waves me out, and as I stand, I look at that poster

again. I wish I knew what it was I should learn, because I know that I should know a lot more than I do.

She sighs as I leave her office and I know she's tired of me.

Even I'm tired of me.

As I run from the office, the hallways are filling with kids. I head back to my classroom to apologize to Mrs. Hall before the buses leave. I run up behind her, tap her on the shoulder.

When she turns and looks at me, her face goes sad before straightening out. I stand there thinking how sorry I am. Hoping she doesn't think I'd wish anything bad on her baby.

But I can't find the words. My mind does the Etch A Sketch thing. Blank.

"What is it, Ally?" she finally asks. She puts her hands on her big belly like she needs to protect it.

I turn and run out of the room. Down the hall and out the front door. The buses are pulling away without me. But that's the way it should be, I guess. I deserve to walk.

All that long way. And all by myself.

CHAPTER 4

Bird in a Cage

When I finally get to Park Road, I head into A. C.
Petersen Farms, which is a weird name for a restaurant.
They have pictures of cows inside and outside but it's
on a busy street with tons of stores. I wonder if there is a
restaurant somewhere in the middle of nowhere named
Crowded City.

My mom is waiting. "Where have you been? I've been
worried sick," she says, wiping her hands on her apron.

"I missed the bus and had to walk."

She shakes her head. "Sit yourself right down there
and start that homework of yours," she says, nodding toward the end of the counter. The same place I always sit.
A place where she can keep an eye on me, she says.

"Anything you want to tell me?" She seems tired.

"They called you, didn't they?" I ask.

"Yes. I don't know why you would do such a thing, Ally." She sounds sad instead of mad. Which is worse, I think.

There is a tray full of glass sundae dishes filled with brightly colored ice cream. Strawberry, pistachio, black raspberry. Pink, green, and purple. I like the colors next to each other and wonder what kind of impossible things I can draw about ice cream. Maybe melting rivers of it. And a man with a cone-shaped head sitting in a banana split dish rowing with a spoon.

"*Ally!* Are you *listening?*"

"Oh. Sorry," I mumble, pushing off the floor with my foot to spin on the padded stool.

"I just don't know what to say anymore."

My mom's boss looks at her over his glasses.

She drops to a whisper. "Just do your homework. We'll talk at home. And please—no spinning on that stool."

"I'm sorry. I am. I really thought Mrs. Hall would like that card."

"How could *that* be?" she says as she picks up the tray of ice cream and moves away.

I pull out a book and open it, but the letters squiggle and dance. How are other people able to read letters that move?

So instead I stare at the steaming liquid dripping into a coffeepot and start thinking of steaming volcanoes. And dinosaurs standing around drinking coffee, staring up at the giant meteor soaring through the air, commenting on how pretty it is. And I think about how lucky they were that they never had to go to school. I grab a napkin and begin a drawing of them for the Sketchbook of Impossible Things.

Soon, my mom's brown and white checkered apron is in front of me.

I look up. "I swear it. I didn't know it was a sym . . . a sym . . . a card for dead people."

"It's a sympathy card," she says. "And it's for the people that miss the person that has died. Not for the dead."

"Well, don't you think the dead person deserves a card more than anyone?"

And she laughs. She leans her elbow on the counter and lifts her other arm to put her hand on my face. It's warm and I'm so relieved that she isn't that mad at me. "You're funny. You know that?"

Then she pulls over the napkin with the dinosaurs holding coffee cups. "What's this?"

"Just an idea I have for the Sketchbook of Impossible Things."

She stares at it. "Aw, your grandpa knew you were

talented, and he'd be so proud of how hard you're working on your art. And he would love that you named your
sketchbook after *Alice in Wonderland*. He had such fun
sharing that book with you." She looks up at me. "Just
like he shared it with me when I was young."

Alice in Wonderland—a book about living in a world
where nothing makes sense made *perfect* sense to me.

"I miss Grandpa," I say. Three words that hold sadness
like a tree holds leaves.

"Me too, sweetheart."

"I miss how he'd move from place to place with us
whenever Dad got stationed somewhere new or deployed. It's weird to think he doesn't know that we've
moved again."

She taps the end of my nose. "I don't know, sweetheart. I think he knows."

Just then, voices I recognize come through the glass
doors. It's Shay and Jessica.

When I turn around, Shay says, "Well, *look* who's here.
It's Ally Nickerson."

They know my mom works here and have seen me here
before. So I figure it isn't a coincidence that they're here.

"Ally," Shay says. "You never came back to class. We
were worried about you."

What a joke *that* is. I turn back around while they

whisper. Then Jessica asks, "Why don't you come sit with us?" Her voice reminds me of a pin hidden inside a candy bar.

My mom motions with her head that I should follow them. "Go ahead, sweetheart. You can take a break."

I give my mom the please-just-stop eyes while Shay mimics the word "sweetheart" in a baby voice.

I guess my mom didn't hear, because she whispers, "New friends would be good, Ally. It wouldn't hurt you to at least give them a chance."

Someone comes to seat them, but Shay asks, "Can we just sit at the counter?"

Great.

Once they sit, there are two stools between them and me.

My mom leans in and whispers, "Why don't you move down and sit with them? They're reaching out, Ally."

Reaching out with a bottle of poison.

I think back to one of our apartments where the landlords kept llamas in their field. I loved them, but Mom said they smelled. I whisper back, "It's more likely that you'd buy me my own pet llama than me sit with them."

She half smiles. "What shall we name the llama?"

I squint and shake my head.

She makes that exasperated sound. "So stubborn."

Shay and Jessica stare at us like two cats watching birds in a cage.

My mom takes her pad out and walks over to them. "Hello, girls. What can I get you?"

Jessica orders strawberry ice cream, but when Shay orders chocolate, Jessica tells my mom, "Oh, that sounds good. I'll have chocolate instead." I roll my eyes. Typical Jessica.

As soon as my mom is gone, Shay asks, "So, Ally?"

I look over.

"Why would you give Mrs. Hall that card? That's, like, really mean."

Since there is no good answer to give, I stare at the page in my book. I'll ignore them. I've taken their teasing before.

Jessica laughs. "Has your mother always been a *waitress*?"

"No," I blurt out. "She used to be an *astronaut*."

They break into laughter and, over near the kitchen, my mom smiles. She thinks I'm bonding with them.

"My father," Jessica begins, "owns his own flower business, and he says—"

Shay interrupts. "Ally, maybe you can be a waitress when you grow up. But can you read the flavors of ice cream for me? I'm having trouble." She points up at the slow-turning cube hanging from the ceiling that lists the flavors on each side. The movement makes it even harder to read.

I feel my face get hot. Oh *no*. Do they know I can't read?

As they laugh, I remember how I had to read aloud last year when I first got here. I knew I shouldn't have, but some stupid voice in my head sometimes says it will be different this time and I try. And I always fail. That day, I read that macaroni can swim up to twenty miles an hour. It was supposed to be a manatee. The class laughed, of course. But so did the teacher, so I tried to pretend I had done it on purpose.

I get up, walk behind them, around the corner and into the back room. I'm not supposed to be back there but it's the only place they can't follow me. I step behind the tall metal shelves with cans of pickles and ketchup and relish that are bigger than my head. Pushing my back hard against the wall, I see words on everything that surrounds me. Boxes and cans and giant plastic bottles.

Words. I can never get away from them.

I think back to second grade when my teacher wrote a whole lot of letters down and asked me what they said. I had no idea. But I was used to that.

"That spells your *name*, Ally. Ally Nickerson."

Who knew a second grader could understand what being humiliated feels like.

Tears begin to come, but I swallow them because I know I'll be found soon. I worry so much about them knowing my secret that my stomach feels like I've been kicked in the guts.

"Ally?" my mom asks as she comes around the corner. "Your friends have gone. What are you doing back here?"

I can't tell her. Thinking I have friends makes her so happy.

"Honey?"

"I was checking the ingredients of ketchup."

Her eyebrows bunch up. She knows something is up, but I walk past her before she asks another question. I walk back out into the restaurant with her following and sit next to Shay's and Jessica's matching empty dishes. It feels like they should mean something. Like maybe I'm an empty dish compared to everyone else.

But mostly those dishes make me feel like this year will be the worst year I've had so far. And that's really saying something.

CHAPTER 5

Silver Dollars and Wooden Nickels

The back door swings open and my brother, Travis, is there, smelling like grease. Looking like he rolled in it. And I instantly feel better.

"How's my favorite little sister?"

"I'm your *only* little sister."

"Doesn't matter. You'd *still* be my favorite." He smiles. "So, your favorite big brother had a silver dollar day today!"

I think of Grandpa and Dad, who always asked us if we were having a silver dollar day or a wooden nickel one.

Travis is doing that thing where he wiggles his fingers in the air and asks his daily question, "What are *these*?" He looks older—more like my dad, who's been deployed since just before Thanksgiving last year. It was hard to feel thankful after he'd gone. Especially since Grandpa had died three months before that.

"The hands of a genius?" I say.

"Correcto-mundo!"

"Do you realize you come home every day and ask me to compliment you?"

"Not really," he says, opening the fridge. "Just asking you to state the facts."

"You are unbelievable."

"*Exactly!*" he says, pointing at me. "Guess what? I finished restoring an old Coke machine today. Thing is like seventy years old." He pops open a soda. "Those things are worth a bundle fixed up." Then he holds up the can. "Look at this. Disappointing compared to those old green bottles."

Travis must be happy. The happier he is, the more he goes on about things.

"*And,*" he says, "I picked up an old gumball machine. The kind that takes pennies. I'll sell it for ten times what I paid for it." His voice drops and he takes a sip. "I will have to throw some money and elbow grease at it first, though."

He comes over like he's going to mess up my hair, but I block his dirty hands. "No way!" I laugh. "Don't touch me!"

"Aw, c'mon, Al. I've had a great day. And guess what?

I almost have enough to buy those rolling tool cabinets. And someday my big neon sign." He sweeps his hand through the air like he's showing me a row of mountains. "*Nickerson Restoration*. My own place. My name—*our* name—is going to be in lights someday, Al." But then his voice deflates. "I just have to get out of high school. We're like oil and water, school and me. I wish Mom would let me quit."

"She would kill you."

"Yeah. So would Dad. And being dead won't be good for my business." He smiles. "Won't be long, though. I'm learning a ton at the garage. The boss is letting me do all kinds of different stuff."

I smile.

"I'm going to buy a car soon, too. A classic. And a V-6 at least."

And then he's off and I can still smell the grease after he's gone.

I'm glad he had a silver dollar day.

When my mom finally gets home, I've already microwaved my dinner and I'm watching TV while I sketch pictures of a pet llama named Butch Cassidy. With a name like that, I give him a cowboy hat, a bandana, and a holster. But in the holster he carries an ear of corn.

When my mom comes in from work, she turns off the TV and I can feel it coming.

"So," she begins. "When are we going to really talk about today?"

"On my ninety-fifth birthday."

"Funny one." She shifts her weight. "I'm trying to be patient, honey. I really am. But today was a *party*. How could you get into trouble at a *party*?"

"I don't have to do anything. They all hate me," I blurt out.

"I doubt that. But can't you see why they'd be tired of your behavior? These shocking things you do and say to get laughs?"

She doesn't get it. Being funny when you don't mean to be is terrible. Having to laugh at yourself along with everyone else is humiliating.

"Oh, Ally . . . you're too smart for this. School is too important to joke about. I don't want you working long hours on your feet for a bunch of tips like me. I want more for you. And you're so smart. Good at math. A gifted artist. Don't you think it's time to stop clowning around?"

"I'm not that smart. You say that, but I'm not."

"Now, we know that isn't true. You could stand to work a little harder, though."

I'm so tired of this conversation. We've had it a hundred times, even though my third-grade teacher told her that I might just be slow, that my mom shouldn't expect too much of me. My mom's eyes got all wide and shiny when she heard that, and I felt sad and embarrassed for her having to be my mom.

But my mother's never bought what that teacher said. I sometimes wish she would, but most times I'm grateful that she hasn't.

She bends over to look me dead in the eyes. "I know that moving as much as we have has been hard for you. And I know I work all the time and can't keep tabs on your schoolwork. It has made it hard for you to keep up with some subjects, and I understand that. I really do. But you're going to have to make more effort, Ally. Things worth having are worth working for."

"I'll do better," I tell her. I used to say this and mean it. Now it feels like I'm just making up one of my stories.

Her smile is sad. "Okay, then." She kisses the top of my head.

"Can I turn the TV back on now?"

She unties her apron as she stares. "Did you take your bath yet?"

"No." I sigh. The tiredness in her voice says there's no use arguing. I trudge toward the hallway.

"By the way, I don't want to hear you say that people hate you," she calls out. "How could anyone on earth possibly hate *you?*"

I wish she could understand my world. But it would be like trying to explain to a whale what it's like to live in the forest.

CHAPTER 6

Triple-Sided Coin

Travis opens the door of the pawn shop in town and waves me in ahead of him. The bell on the door announces our arrival as it hits the glass. The dusty smell of the place triggers a bunch of memories. Good times. Together times. When Dad and Grandpa would take Travis and me out looking for coins. Numbers and money are something Travis and I can do well. So we took to it fast.

Grandpa loved the dustiest stores best because they were the ones that would have uncracked rolls of coins in the backs of their safes. When the store owners would trade the old rolls for new bills, we'd open them at home to see what was inside. Sometimes we'd find a buffalo nickel, a Mercury dime, or an Indian head penny. It was like a little bit of Christmas. Being here makes me ache to go back in time.

The man behind the counter doesn't say hello. He rolls a toothpick back and forth in his mouth with his tongue. In one way it is completely impressive, and in another, the grossest thing I've ever seen.

Travis rests his fingertips on the glass counter, looking down into the case filled with coins.

"You need something?" The man doesn't talk the way Mom says you're supposed to talk to customers.

"I want to buy some coins," Travis says.

"Oh, yeah?"

"Yeah." Travis brushes his chin with his knuckle—something he does when he is nervous.

The guy reaches up and takes the toothpick out of his mouth. He uses it to point at Travis. "Do you have money or are you all talk?"

Travis does what Dad said never to do. He shows him his money. And not money like a regular person. A roll of money wrapped in an elastic band.

The guy's eyes widen. Then he asks, "Looking for something special?"

"I want liberty coins. You got any?"

He takes out several coins. One is a Mercury dime with a head that looks like it has wings for ears. "I remember those!" I say. "Like the one Daddy has in his wallet."

Travis turns them over in his hand. "Nice. You have anything more unusual?"

The guy's eyebrows jump. He reaches into a drawer. "This is unusual, but it'll cost you big."

"I don't mind paying for something special."

"Okay, then," he says. "This one is special." He puts a penny on the counter.

Travis picks it up and his eyebrows bunch up. "This is smaller than other pennies."

The guy nods. "It is. A rare find."

Travis glances at me, and then he turns toward the guy. "How much?"

"Well," the guy says, "if you know anything about coins, you know that a coin with a flaw in it is far more valuable than a regular coin."

Something isn't right with it and it's worth *more*?

"Like I said," Travis says, "how much?"

The guy tilts his head to the side. "Well, normally I'd ask for eighty, but I'll charge you . . . say . . . seventy-five?"

Travis smiles. Even I remember how Dad used to tell us never to smile when you get a number. Never. Even if it's the best number in the world—and here he is smiling like he won the lottery. I try to look serious enough for the both of us.

"Well, that's really generous of you. Seventy-five bucks for a penny that's been dipped in nitric acid."

The guy's smile falls off of his face.

"I bet the police would be interested in a little bit of fraud."

"Now, listen—"

Travis interrupts. "Look, I wasn't born yesterday. Stop messing with me." Travis points at a coin in the case that has a walking woman wrapped in a sheet with the sun's rays behind her. It is beautiful. "That 1933 Walking Liberty half dollar. How much for that one?"

"Well, that one is in really fine condition. In fact . . ."

"Just tell me how much," Travis says, leaning in, palms on the glass.

"Forty-five."

"Thirty-six and you throw in the Mercury dime for my little sister."

I look up quick. For me?

Then I do the math. Yup. He is following Dad's rule of offering 20 percent less than what they offer. But Travis threw in something extra.

The guy squints. "Forty."

Travis nods. "Done." He slaps the money on the glass case.

Outside the store, Travis holds the dime toward me.

"Oh, it's beautiful! I love it so much. Thank you, Travis! You're the best!"

He looks a little sad staring at the coin. "You know,

Grandpa was born in 1933. That's why I chose these coins. They were both minted in that year."

I look down at my Mercury dime and its date, wishing people could last as long as coins.

When we get into the car, Travis says, "Did you see how that guy in there took me for a fool? Trying to rip me off. Remember, Ally. When people have low expectations of you, you can sometimes use it to your advantage." Then he looks me right in the eyes and points at my nose. "As long as *you* don't have low expectations of yourself. You hear?"

I nod again. But I think to myself that it's hard not to these days.

CHAPTER 7

No Grandpas Here

I sit on my bed, holding my copy of *Alice in Wonderland*. The shaky writing in the front of the book says, "For Ally—my wondrous girl! Love, Grandpa." The colors of the book are all bright even though the book is old. Inside, the pages are soft and the writing is bigger than in books now. But I still can't read it by myself. It's like having a gift that's locked in a glass box.

I'm feeling heavy, but I always do on Sunday nights. The thought of another week of school does that. It's like knowing I have to pull a tire through a keyhole the next day.

But I'll have a new teacher. A *Mr. Daniels* sounds

like a grandfatherly type with pockets full of lollipops, which could be nice. I'm hoping he'll spend a lot of time straightening his bow tie and telling us about the good ol' days and not giving us much work.

But when I show up, I find that Mr. Daniels is no grandfather. He's younger than Mrs. Hall. He wears a dark jacket and a tie with colored circles on it. When I get closer, I realize they're planets.

Most of the kids are gathered around him. I throw my stuff in the closet and walk over. He says, "My very excellent mother just served us nachos," and claims it is an easy way to memorize the planets in order from the sun.

Albert, whose hair reminds me of a bird's nest, stands nearby. "I feel bad for Pluto."

I look over and my eyes are pulled to the bruises on his arms.

"Pluto was a planet all those years and then someone just decided it wasn't anymore? Too small. Too far away. Orbit not just right."

"I don't really think Pluto cares, Albert," I mumble.

He sits in his chair and says, "Well, *I* do."

I feel bad for him and want to ask him about the marks. He is big and clunky but not fat. The kind of size where others would usually leave him alone.

I pull out my chair and sit down. Okay, I tell myself.

I'm going to do better. I'm going to work harder. That's all I need to do. I'm going to really concentrate this time. Even though I know I've tried that and it doesn't work.

Reading for me is like when I drop something and my fingers scramble to catch it and just when I think I've got it, I don't. If *trying* to read helped, I'd be a genius.

Mr. Daniels is in front of me. I hold my breath and lean back. He holds out his hand. "I'm Mr. Daniels. Nice to meet you," he says.

Shay leans toward Jessica. "I guess he doesn't know who he's talking to." As usual, most of her friends laugh.

"Hey," Mr. Daniels says, turning to her. "That isn't cool. We don't do that in here." Which wipes the smile off Shay's face. Then he turns back to me. "What's your name?"

"Ally Nickerson," I answer, so softly that even I can barely hear myself.

"Well, are you going to shake my hand, Ally Nicker-son?" he asks. "I don't bite on Mondays."

Great. Just what I need. A funny guy for a teacher. I take his hand, but only for a second. My mind is already spinning off. Wondering what terrible things Mrs. Silver has told him. The plans they've made for me. I see myself wrapped in rope and lying on the train tracks just like in Grandpa's old black-and-white silent movies.

"Okay, Fantasticos! Take your seats!" he calls. "Time to set the world on fire!"

Everyone scrambles to their seats, but I'm still lying on the imaginary train tracks. All tied up and watching the engine come around the corner.

CHAPTER 8

Real Trouble

The first day with Mr. Daniels starts out okay be-cause we have math in the morning and Mr. Daniels does this thing he calls the bus driver. He says, "You're the bus driver." And then he tells us how many people get on and off and we have to add and subtract the numbers in our head. No paper. No pencils. Just math.

When I was younger, I loved math. Everything about math. But in school, math now has letters. Like what does x equal? There are also long stories with characters, and although the story is supposed to end with some number, all the words block my path to getting there.

But the day turns into a wooden nickel day at snack time, when Mr. Daniels calls me up to his desk. He holds the assignment that I did for Mrs. Hall where we had to describe ourselves, the one with "Why?" written over and over on it. My stomach flops over.

"So, I'm wondering what this means, exactly. Can you tell me?" he asks.

I shrug.

"I'm wondering if you can write just one paragraph for me. Something about you. I'd like to learn something about you."

I stay quiet. With teachers, if you stay quiet long enough, they start doing the talking for you. Filling in the answers and then you just have to nod. So I wait.

But he waits, too.

Finally, he says, "C'mon, now. Can you write that paragraph for me?"

I feel heavy. "No," I say.

He doesn't want to know about the real me. It'll be like people in scary movies who think they want to know what's in the basement, but when they find out, they're always sorry.

"Ally? Did you say no?" he asks, without being mad.

I turn myself to stone.

He takes a deep breath and leans forward. "So, is it writing you don't like?"

I think about saying no, except it could cause me trouble later. Like the chess games in Grandpa's *Alice in*

Wonderland book. You have to be super sure before you make a move final. But I figure Mr. Daniels probably already knows this about me, so I nod.

"What do you like, then?"

"Buffalo wings," I say.

He laughs a little. "What do you like about school?"

"Leaving."

He waits for me to say more.

"I like math. And art. I like to draw."

"Oh, well, that's cool. Do you draw a lot?"

"Yeah."

"So, do you find the writing difficult or do you just not like it?"

"It's easy," I lie. "It's just boring."

"Well, maybe we can do some things to make it less boring for you. To excite you about writing. It's a great way to explore. Be creative. Ask questions."

I point at my paper. "I asked lots of questions there."

"Yes." He laughs. "I guess you did."

He takes a deep breath. "Here's the thing, Ally. I'm going to be honest with you. I've talked with both Mrs. Hall and Mrs. Silver. I know that you have spent a lot of time in the office in the past. You're good at getting sent to the office, but you know, you can be too good at the wrong things."

Uh-oh.

"I just want you to know that I'm going to try really hard not to send you to the office. If we have something to deal with, you and I will deal with it together." He winks. "What happens in room 206 stays in room 206."

What?

"So, we won't involve Mrs. Silver anymore, okay? I think she has enough to do around here."

Oh no. Did he just take away my "Get Out of Jail Free" card?

"Also," he says, moving his head to look me in the eye, "I'm on your side, okay? I want to help you."

So he wants to help me, huh? He has no idea what he's in for.

CHAPTER 9

Bag Full of Nothing

Today, we're each supposed to bring in something that represents us and tell the class about it. I thought of a few things I could bring, like a can full of dirt or a bag full of nothing.

Mr. Daniels asks for volunteers to go first. Shock of the century when Shay raises her hand.

She gets up there with a picture of her horse, Diamond. She goes on about how she loves him and goes riding several times a week but how it's a lot of work to take care of him. She shows us her riding helmet and fancy riding jacket, too. I guess there really isn't anything that she doesn't have.

Jessica brings a picture of Shay and talks about what

43

good friends they are, which I think is funny since we're supposed to talk about ourselves.

Oliver bounces to the front of the room. His feet are never on the floor at the same time. He takes out a lightbulb. "I. Am. The giver of LIGHT!"

"*Really?*" Mr. Daniels asks.

"Well, my dad is. He sells lamps. And when I grow up I'm going to be a salesman, too. I'm going to sell hangers."

"Hangers?" Mr. Daniels asks.

"Yeah! Because I was thinking that it should be something that everyone has, because you'd want to sell stuff that most people need, because if you sold stuff that nobody wanted, then you wouldn't sell anything, right? And everybody needs hangers."

Mr. Daniels smiles and puts his hand on Oliver's shoulder. "Oliver, you are one clever boy. You know that?"

I haven't been in this school that long, but I'm going to guess that Oliver hasn't heard that said much. He falls into his chair, which tips back, but he grabs his desk, rights himself, and cheers for his own victory.

Albert gets up next. As always, he wears the shirt with *Flint* on it and his bruises. He reaches into a brown paper lunch bag and pulls out a jar of clear liquid.

He clears his throat. "This is a mixture of two parts hydrogen and one part oxygen molecules."

"Will it explode?" yells Oliver.

Albert does not answer. Instead, he unscrews the metal lid and drinks whatever it is. I'm silently freaked out, but Oliver goes nuts. "He drank it! Did you see that? He drank molecules! *Gross!*"

"It is merely water," Albert reports.

While Mr. Daniels speaks to Albert, Shay whispers to Jessica, "Water? Really? That's all he's got?"

Shay has gotten even better at being mean. Ever since Mr. Daniels kept her in for recess for making fun of Oliver, she saves her comments for when Mr. Daniels is busy or talking to someone else.

"This water was taken from a giant underground lake that goes on for miles and miles," Albert announces. "It's the same water that the dinosaurs walked through a hundred million years ago and the cavemen drank. It's the same water that polar bears swam in just last year and medieval knights guzzled after battle."

Oliver and most of the other boys stand, trying to get a better look.

"That's cool, Albert!" Max says. "Where did you get it?"

Jessica and Shay smile and lean forward to look at Max. Shay calls out, "Yeah, Albert. Where did you get it?"

"I got it from my kitchen faucet."

Huh?

"The same water has been here and been reused since the Earth began. It is important to me because, as a scientist and historian, I know that we are but a blip on the Earth's timeline. A grain of sand on an entire beach of time."

Kids are starting to groan. "Here goes the professor again," Max says.

"Yeah. Such a showoff," Jessica says, turning to Max.

"Now, knock that off," Mr. Daniels says. "I think Albert's idea is fascinating. How Earth has recycled its water over and over. Extraordinary, Albert!"

Next, he calls on Keisha. She carries a small box and holds it like whatever is inside will break easily. When she takes out a cupcake, the boys argue about who'll get to eat it.

"This is a cupcake that I made. It isn't from a box mix; it's homemade."

"And why is it important to you?" Mr. Daniels asks.

"I like to bake. I told my mom I want to start a business when I get older, and she said there's no time like the present. So this is the first one I'll show to anyone outside my family."

"My God," Shay whispers. "She acts like she's the first to make a cupcake. It's not even decorated or anything."

"Shay. Please keep your comments constructive," Mr. Daniels says.

"Yes, it is plain on the outside," Keisha says, half smiling at Shay, "but it's the inside that matters."

Keisha takes a knife out of her box and cuts the cupcake in half and shows us the inside. "As you can see, it says 'yum' on the inside."

"How did you do that?" Suki asks, and I'm surprised to hear her talk. She hardly ever says anything.

"I've been experimenting with making letters out of different kinds of dough. I stand the letters up in the cupcake batter and carefully cover them with more batter."

"Do you lick the spoon when you're done?" Oliver asks. "I like to lick the spoon, but my mom says too much sugar isn't good for me, so she doesn't bake much because—"

"Oliver," Mr. Daniels says, pulling on his own ear. Oliver stops right away.

Then Mr. Daniels looks at the cupcake. "Wow, Keisha. That is pretty impressive!"

"I'm going to call my baking business 'Hidden Messages'—the *batter* way to send a note."

"That's fantastic, Keisha," Mr. Daniels says. "The possibilities are infinite."

Albert raises his hand and Mr. Daniels points to him. "The possibilities are not, in fact, infinite, as she would eventually run out of appropriate letter combinations, and the number of letters to be used in each cake would be limited as well. Also, you imply that the possibilities are all positive when it is probable that the possibilities would be equal in positive and negative outcomes."

"Actually, you're correct, Albert," Mr. Daniels says. "But I am an optimist. What can I say?"

"So you agree that the possibilities aren't endless?"

"Well, I agree from a mathematical standpoint, Albert, but not from a human one. I believe that the things we put numbers on are not necessarily the things that count the most. You can't measure the stuff that makes us human. Like Keisha's creativity or how hard she'll work." Mr. Daniels shrugs. "Just my opinion."

"Well, it seems that the part that can be measured is most important," Albert says. "Because that's what can be proven."

"Well, my fine young fellow, I think we'll have to agree to disagree," Mr. Daniels says, walking by Albert and patting his shoulder.

Then Mr. Daniels calls on Suki. She pulls out tiny paper bags and begins to pass them out to everyone.

"I bring two foods to share. One is *hone-senbei*, my grandfather favorite. Other is wasabi peas. They are maybe spicy. Food in America tastes . . ." She turns to Mr. Daniels. "What is correct word?"

All of a sudden Max jumps up and runs to the sink, followed by Keisha and Jessica. "Too hot!" Max yells. The three push each other a bit, trying to scoop water into their mouths.

"Ah yes," Suki continues. "*Bland* is correct word. Food

here is *bland*." She seems to think that the three kids at the sink are both funny and odd.

I think how hard it would be to move to a different country and have to learn another language. I can't even handle one.

Mr. Daniels laughs, holding the little bumpy, bright green pea between his fingers. "They don't *look* that hot."

Most people in the class are too chicken to eat it now, pushing it away. Suki looks a little hurt.

Albert puts one in his mouth. He eats it but looks like he's in pain. His eyes even water. He says with a gasp, "I like it, Suki. Thank you."

That Albert is nice.

Oliver pops his in his mouth but has no reaction.

"Oliver?" Mr. Daniels asks. "You don't think it's hot?"

"Naw! I'm the only one in my family that can finish a fireball without taking it out of my mouth. My mother says I must have no taste buds at all, and my dad says—"

Mr. Daniels pulls on his earlobe again and says, "Thanks, Oliver."

Oliver's mouth is open. Ready to keep going. But he says, "Thanks, Mr. Daniels." Do they have some signal or something?

Suki continues. "These foods mean much to me because I share them with Grandfather. Many things about Japan I miss, but Grandfather I most miss. Also, I miss wood carving with him. He make me wooden blocks and I carve gift for him and send."

So that's why she has those blocks.

"I eat these foods because they remind me of Japan. And my grandfather."

I feel sad for her.

"What are the crackers made of?" asks Albert.

Suki turns to him. "They are made of shrimp and fish bones."

It isn't just Oliver who goes wild over that one. Most everyone says "Yuck," and Suki looks up at Mr. Daniels, who turns to the class. "Now, now. Quiet down."

"Shrimp and fish bones?" Shay asks. "We prefer lobster in our family."

Albert raises his hand. "I would just like to point out that lobster is a very expensive meal now, but in the olden days, it was served only to peasants and slaves, who revolted and demanded that they only be served lobster twice a week. And"—he swallows—"I think fish bones would have some excellent nutritional properties."

Suki smiles for a second before she scurries back to her seat. Mr. Daniels gives Albert a solid nod.

Next, it's my turn. What I ended up bringing in means something to me, but now I'm not sure the class would be nice about it. I decide to play it safe and say I forgot.

I can tell Mr. Daniels is disappointed. "Well then, do you have a pet you can tell us about?" he asks.

"No. My mom is allergic." This reminds me of my dad crawling around the living room on all fours, pretending to be the puppy I begged for.

Oliver starts to bark like a dog.

Mr. Daniels says, "Too much of that, Oliver, and we'll have to give you dog biscuits. Better be careful."

Mr. Daniels squints at me. "Are you *sure* there's nothing you can show us? Because I have a feeling there's something."

I slide my hand down into my pocket and clutch my 1943 steel penny. The object I brought in for sharing today.

He watches my hand and I realize I've given myself away. So I stand and I take out the penny.

"My dad is in the army and he's deployed right now. On the day my dad left, he gave Travis and me these pennies." I look up at Mr. Daniels. "That's my big brother."

He nods.

"In 1943, pennies looked weird because they were silver in color like quarters. They were made of steel instead of copper because the government needed copper to make ammunition during World War Two. Then in 1944, pennies went back to the usual red copper color. Anyway, I think it's cool."

"I do, too," Mr. Daniels says. "And I think it's even more cool that you told us about it."

As I walk back to my seat, I think of how when Dad left, he said that when we look at the steel pennies, we need to remember that we are unique, too. And also, that things will go back to normal for us—that he'll be home before we know it.

I really miss him.

Mr. Daniels gives Oliver a thumbs-up, and I think how cool it is that they have the ear-pulling signal. That way he doesn't always have to tell Oliver that he's doing something wrong in front of everyone. I know what that feels like and I'm happy that Mr. Daniels cares so much. Most teachers seem to like their students to be all the same—perfect and quiet. Mr. Daniels actually seems to like that we're different.

CHAPTER 10

Promises, Promises . . .

"All right, Fantasticos!" Mr. Daniels says, rubbing his hands together like a mad scientist. "First thing I'm going to do today is book talk. I will do that a lot this year—tell you all about some of my favorite stories."

When Mr. Daniels talks about books, it reminds me of Max or Oliver. Like he's ready to launch a giant party. I like hearing about the story. But asking me to read them would be like asking a lobster to play tennis.

And then it gets worse.

He holds up a pile of notebooks. "I have a surprise. I have a brand-new writing journal for each of you, which you will write in every day."

Oh no. I'd rather eat grass.

"But here's the thing. I will sometimes give you a topic but not very often. And I will never ever—even if an evil sorcerer threatens to turn all my correcting pens to clear ink—correct your work."

Huh?

"They will never be graded. They will never be corrected. And most days, I won't tell you what to write about. You may write about your life, sports, the country of Bulgaria, your favorite kind of soap, books you like, books you don't like. *Anything.*"

Wow. I wonder if he's delirious. No correcting? Anything we want? This is too good to be true; I know something is coming.

"There are only a couple of rules."

Ah. *There* they are. The *rules.*

"You must put pencil to paper and do *something.* And I will often answer with a sentence or two."

"Write back?" Oliver asks. "Can we grade *you*?"

Mr. Daniels laughs. "We're not going to grade at all, Oliver. This is about communication. Self-expression. Not measurements."

"Can we ask you questions?" Max asks.

"Sure!" he says, passing out the notebooks. Mine is yellow. A little too nice a color for a writing thing.

"Can I write about football?" Max asks.

"Anything you want."

"This is going to be great!" Oliver yells. "I'm going to ask for answers to the tests. And for extra recesses. And unlimited ketchup in the cafeteria."

"Well," Mr. Daniels begins, "as I said, you can *ask* whatever you want." He smiles at Oliver. "So, open up those notebooks now and add your first entry. And make it . . . *you*. This journal is yours, so an introduction to you may be a good thing—no matter how you choose to express that."

Keisha begins writing while Albert stares at the blank page. The room is filled with the sounds of pencils scratching.

Suki is rubbing one of her blocks with her thumb. I wonder if she's thinking about her grandfather.

I see a mind movie of me walking through a forest of alphabet blocks stacked on top of each other. They sway like trees in the wind and I worry that they will come crashing down on me.

I think about drawing that, but decide to color a big three-dimensional cube with dark black sides. He said we could do anything. I want to see if he means it.

The next day Mr. Daniels holds my journal, opened to the page where I drew the black cube.

I figured he wouldn't let that go.

He holds his palm facing me and says, "I know. I know

I said I'd never correct you and I'm not going to. I'm just wondering if you would mind telling me what this means. Do you like the color black, or does it mean something? Either way, it's okay."

I think of the kinds of things that might make him mad and remember how he said a person can be too good at the wrong things. Maybe I don't want to get in trouble this time.

"It's a picture of a dark room."

"Oh. Why would you draw a picture of a dark room?" He looks serious now.

"It was supposed to be something about us."

"Why would a dark room have something to do with you, Ally?" His voice is soft. Really soft.

I swallow hard. "Because in a dark room, no one could see me."

He stares down at my black cube. Then he clears his throat before looking back up. "Okay. Thank you for being honest, Ally."

I'm so relieved he isn't mad.

"Ally?" He pauses. "Can you tell me why you don't want to be seen?"

"I think it would be easier to be invisible."

"Why?"

I shrug. I want to give him an answer, but I have both too many words and not enough.

He nods slowly. "Well," he says. "I'm glad you're not invisible, Ally. Because this class wouldn't be the same without you."

I don't believe him, but it makes me happy he said it.

I realize looking at him that, all this time, I haven't been looking teachers in the face. I've been staring into their stomachs while I sit at my desk and they tell me the things that are wrong with me.

But now, on top of all those other big wishes that I carry around, I have one more. I want to impress Mr. Daniels. With every tiny little piece of myself, I just want him to like me.

CHAPTER 11

Scrambled Egg

When we come into the classroom, Mr. Daniels makes an announcement. "Attention, Fantasticos! We have brand-new fantastico seats. So, find yours and settle in."

Jessica is sitting next to Suki and staring at Shay like their separation is a great injustice.

It turns out that I'm sitting in the front row next to Keisha—the girl who can bake and write at the same time while I can't do either.

We don't speak all morning, and I can't stop worrying that she doesn't like me. When she finally glances at me, I blurt out, "I don't mind being your friend."

Keisha looks annoyed. "*You* don't have to do *me* any favors."

"No," I say, trying to undo what I didn't mean to say. "I just mean . . ." And then I stop because I don't know what I meant and I'm nervous and embarrassed and that is never good when I'm trying to say something. Every word is another shovelful of dirt from the hole I've dug for myself. So I figure my best bet is to shut my mouth.

But the silence gets too long and too loud, so I try to think of something to say. I always knew what to say to my grandpa and he always knew what to say to me. I wish he were here to whisper in my ear. And then I think of Alice and how she argued with Humpty Dumpty about using the right words. I turn to Keisha and blurt out, "Do you like eggs?"

"*Eggs?*" she asks.

Oh no. She thinks I'm a barrel full of crazy, but I keep going because sometimes my tongue goes on without my say-so. "Yeah. I love eggs. Scrambled eggs. Fried eggs. Poached on toast, and boiled eggs. I love peeling the shell off of a boiled egg, don't you? I even like egg salad, which my brother won't eat even if someone holds him down . . ."

Her eyebrows scrunch up, reminding me of angry caterpillars. "That's incredibly interesting." Then she searches inside her desk for something. I know this move. It's a polite way of ignoring me. People do it a lot.

Finally, I just put my head down. Grandpa used to say

that Alice in Wonderland falling down the rabbit hole was just like real life. I didn't used to understand what he meant, but I do now.

There can't be any place on the planet scarier than a school cafeteria. I hold my tray so tight, my fingers hurt.

I hear, "Hey, Ally!" It's Shay. She is standing with Jessica and a few others.

"Yeah?" I ask.

"Do you want to sit with us for lunch?"

Of course I don't want to sit with them. But I am getting tired of sitting alone. And having everyone else *see* me sit alone.

Besides that, Shay, Jessica, and some other girls all have these woven friendship bracelets. And I have never had the kinds of friends who have matching bracelets, but I have always wanted them. It's like the bracelet tells the world that the person wearing it has someone who cares about them. Not like a family member that *has* to care, but someone who just likes you.

I want to feel a part of something. Anything, I guess.

Shay is overly happy that I've said yes.

I sit down after glancing at the seat to make sure I won't be sitting in a pool of glue. Shay motions to me to sit next to her. She and Jessica smile that smile that on the outside seems fine but your gut tells you to be careful of. There are a few other girls. Max is there with one other boy.

Jessica points at Albert and they start laughing. I look over and don't see anything funny. "Can you believe it?" Shay asks. "How pathetic is that? Hey, Albert," she calls, "is that supposed to be a fashion statement?"

I still don't get it. He's wearing his usual Flint shirt and jeans. Why are they so worked up now?

Shay hits me on the side of the arm and points down at his feet.

The backs of his sneakers have been cut out.

Shay calls him over and he comes. I don't know why everyone does what she says. Even me. Today, anyway.

"What's the matter?" she asks him. "Don't you have any money for shoes?"

"Quite the contrary," Albert begins. "But given the choice of buying new sneakers that I will outgrow in three months or a chemistry set that I can use for an undefined amount of time, this seemed the clear choice. They're in fine shape except for being just a bit short."

"Did you hear that?" Shay asks. "He chopped the back of his shoes off. Like slippers."

Jessica adds, "Next, he'll be wearing a robe."

Shay turns to her. "I think robes would be cool. We should wear them tomorrow."

"Yeah, that *would* be cool!" Jessica says.

Shay laughs, but I don't think Jessica knows Shay isn't laughing because of the robes. I think Shay said something dumb to see if Jessica would go along. Sometimes I think Jessica would follow Shay out of an airplane without a parachute.

Then Shay turns to me. "Well, Ally," she asks, "what do *you* think of wearing robes tomorrow?"

I'd like to tell her it's dumb, but I say, "Not my thing."

"Is that so? Well, what do you think of Albert and his slippers?"

I feel like I'm in one of those old detective movies that Grandpa loved. In a cramped, small room under a bright light, being asked a question I don't want to answer.

The thought to stick up for him goes through my head, but that doesn't seem like the right answer for Shay.

"They're pretty dopey," I say. "What a weirdo, huh?"

I've made Shay happy.

I feel terrible.

And I know that I am going to feel even worse when the shade comes down over Albert's face. When he looks sad.

But that never comes. He just stands there eating Doritos and studying us like we are lab mice. "I think it curious that you worry about what I have on my feet when three of you are wearing red shirts. Not a wise color. Red is the color of stop lights and signs, bad wounds, warning lights, and the most severe of sunburns. It represents red alerts and high fevers. Red numbers show a loss in accounting. Red represents danger."

I think of all of the red marks that cover my papers from teachers. How I hate to get them back.

Jessica laughs loudest. "What a weirdo, Albert!"

"Furthermore," he says, "any crew member of *Star Trek*'s starship *Enterprise* who wears a red shirt never appears in another episode. Frankly, I think you've made poor choices."

They all burst into loud laughter. "Albert!" Max says. "It's only a TV show, dude. And not a very good one, either."

Albert's arm stops dead on the way to his mouth with another Dorito. "Not a very *good* one?"

"Albert," Shay says, leaning forward a bit, "you go right ahead and ignore what you look like. But it's the rest of us who suffer; *we* have to look at you."

"Actually," he says, "I don't take my appearance lightly. I take *you* lightly."

And with that he turns and is gone before she can pull out some other mean thing. And I wish I was more like Albert. Seeing him shuffle away in those sneakers makes me want to be better. I'm not perfect, but at least I'm not mean.

And then my heart sinks, because I realize that I just was.

I guess I did it because I was lonely. Now I know that there are worse things than being lonely.

CHAPTER 12

What's Your Problem, Albert?

Light from the hallway pours into my room as my mom opens the door. "Hey, honey."

"Hey."

"I came in to check on you. You seemed very quiet at dinner tonight. Something going on?"

"Mean kids at school."

"Oh, Ally Bug. I'm sorry you had to put up with that. What happened?"

"Well . . . the kids who were mean?"

"Yeah?"

"I was kind of one of them."

"Oh," she says with a sigh. "I'm surprised by that, Ally. Tell me what happened."

"Those girls that came into Petersen's that time? Well, they asked me to have lunch with them. I sat at their table but then they started being mean to this kid named Albert about his clothes." I look up into her eyes. "And I went along with it. I feel bad about it."

My mom brushes my forehead with her fingertips. "You're not a little girl anymore, Ally. So it's not too soon to decide what kind of person you want to be. Of course, *I* know what kind of person you are. And I love you for it." She kisses me on the forehead. "You made a mistake. Everyone does. Just do your best to make it right, that's all. The words 'I'm sorry' are powerful ones."

"Yeah. Okay. I'll make it right with him."

"That's my girl," she says, kissing my forehead one more time before leaving.

The next morning at school, I am wondering how I can make things right with Albert. I'm drawing a pigeon wedding in my sketchbook. I don't know that Keisha is standing behind me.

"You drew that?"

I move my arm to cover it.

"Why would you cover it? If I could draw like that, I'd put a commercial on TV about it."

"Thanks," I mumble. I don't know why I'm embarrassed, but I am.

Keisha sits in her chair as I stare at her head full of thin braids, thinking it must take three days to do all that—so beautiful. I just love it. Not like my boring hair that just hangs there. I reach out to touch her hair. She turns toward me all of a sudden. "What are you *doing*?"

"Oh . . . I . . . Sorry. There was a mosquito." Sometimes I can't believe the things I do. It's like my arm has its own brain.

"Uh-huh," Keisha says.

Just then, Albert walks in, and he looks upset. I want to be able to tell my mom that I made things right with him, so I go over.

"Albert? Are you okay?" I ask, wondering if he'll tell me to strap myself to a rocket and light the fuse.

"I have a problem."

"I'm sorry about the cafeteria thing," I blurt out.

His eyebrows rise. "That didn't bother me. No need to apologize."

"It didn't bother you at all to have a table full of people make fun of you? You're kidding."

"Why would I be kidding?"

Can it be that he really doesn't care what people think of him?

We just stare at each other. If that didn't bother him at all and this new problem really does, then it must be really bad. Maybe it has to do with the bruises he has all the time.

"Can I help?" I ask.

"No offense. But I don't really think so."

"Okay," I mumble.

"It's just a problem that I can't get out of my head. I feel like I won't be able to relax until I find an answer."

"Do you want to talk about it? I know sometimes when I have a problem, I talk it out with my brother or mom. Even if I don't find an answer, I feel better anyway."

"Well . . ."

I wait.

"I've just been wondering . . . if an insect is flying inside a moving train car, is it traveling faster than the train itself? And if the insect flies in the opposite direction that the train is moving in, is it then traveling more slowly than the train? Obviously, if the fly is on the wall, it is moving at the same speed. As long as it isn't walking. But the movement within movement is a puzzle to me."

Oh.

He turns to me. A little intense. "You can see the problem here." He doesn't ask. He tells.

I know he doesn't really think I can help. Who knows if I could possibly figure out the science part of what he's talking about. But my mind shows me that insect in that train car.

It's a dragonfly with brilliant greenish-blue wings and tiny goggles over its eyes.

The car is old with dark wood walls and dark green curtains. Like from Grandpa's Westerns. And the people have old-fashioned clothes. I see them like they're with me now. Some of the men are sleeping. One is waving the dragonfly off with a newspaper, not even noticing its tiny goggles. Ladies with the most beautiful dresses sit there, too.

And I see a girl who is with her mother, and her mother keeps asking the girl if she is enjoying the ride and the girl keeps saying yes, being sure to have a happy-sounding voice.

I don't know everything about that girl, but I do know that she has a lot more to worry about than an insect on a train. She doesn't fit in. She's all dressed up in fancy clothes and has to pretend to be someone she's not. She wants to muck around. Help build fences. She wants to ride a horse the real way—not sidesaddle like her mother insists.

When I come back from my mind movie, Albert has already walked away. But I don't care. I can't help thinking about the girl on the train and how she feels—like she wants to do so much but she's held back, and it makes her feel heavy and angry. Like she's dragging a concrete block around all of the time. I'd like to help her break free from that.

CHAPTER 13

Trouble with Flowers

It's the night of the holiday concert, when we sing about Santa and dreidels and Kwanzaa. The best part is getting a new dress.

I stand in front of a mirror looking at my dress and my first shoes with a heel on them. Thinking about the shopping day I had with my mom. We even went to A. C. Petersen's for lunch. I liked how she stayed with me in a booth instead of having to go wait on other people.

I love to sing, but I don't like our music teacher, Mrs. Muldoon. Max calls her Minefield Muldoon because you never can tell when she'll blow up over something. Oliver calls her that, too, but he acts it out by leaping into the air and yelling, "Muldoooooooon!" as he lands on the floor and rolls. He doesn't stop, though. He goes from a roll right to his feet again. Like a cat in a cartoon.

Shay is making fun of Albert because his clothes don't fit. "What's with the pants, Albert?" she says. "Did you get that outfit in the third grade?"

Keisha whips around fast. "Why do you *always* try to pull people down?" she asks.

"Because some people deserve it, that's why," Shay answers.

"*Deserve* to be pulled down? *Really?*" Keisha asks.

Albert straightens his tie, which is the only part of his outfit that fits. He's even wearing his sneakers with the backs cut out. "You know," he says, "logically, if a person was to pull another down, it would mean that he or she is already below that person."

Keisha lets out a laugh so loud that Mrs. Muldoon shoots her a look. Keisha covers her mouth and tries to squelch the sound. "*That* is perfect, Albert. Man, you really are a smart dude." She turns to Shay. "You, on the other hand, are so low, you could play tennis against a curb."

Shay's eyes narrow, but before she can say anything, Mrs. Muldoon appears and tells us to line up.

For the spring concert last year, before I had a growth spurt, I had to stand in the front row. I liked when Travis called me a dime among pennies. But this year, I get to stand toward the back of the line with the taller kids, right next to Keisha. I look over at her. I love how she stuck up for Albert. She had the guts that I didn't in the cafeteria. I wish I could be braver.

We all stand, waiting to file into the auditorium. "Oh, Mrs. Muldoon, I *love* your dress!" Shay says.

Mrs. Muldoon lights up like a bulb. "Why, thank you, Shay. Your parents have raised such a nice young lady."

"Oh, thank you very much, Mrs. Muldoon." Shay smiles, but when she turns away toward Jessica, she rolls her eyes. And she keeps glaring at Keisha.

I decide I won't think about how mad she makes me and I'll think, instead, about how all the girls get to carry a bouquet of flowers. That's the good news. The bad news is that they have been donated by Jessica's father, the florist. It's nice of him, but Jessica hasn't stopped bragging about it.

Mrs. Muldoon walks down the line, handing out the most beautiful bouquets I have ever seen. Like the ones that brides carry. Dark red ribbons that wind around the stems like a barbershop light pole. Ribbons dangle from the bottom, too. She hands my bunch to me, and I smile thinking of how much my mom will love to see me with them.

Keisha leans in to smell them and runs her fingers

over the tops of the flowers. Then one of the white buds falls off and bounces off the top of her shiny black shoe.

Mrs. Muldoon is there in a second. "What do you think you're doing?"

"I just . . ."

Mrs. Muldoon grabs the flowers from Keisha's hands. Keisha looks up. "No. *Please* don't. I didn't mean . . ."

"These flowers are a *gift*, and if that's how you're going to treat a gift—with a complete lack of respect and gratitude—then you, Keisha Almond, will be the *only* girl *without* flowers."

"But Mrs. Muldoon," Keisha says, "I really didn't—"

Mrs. Muldoon holds up her hand like she's stopping traffic. "I *don't* want to hear it. You will have no flowers and perhaps you will remember in the future how a lady behaves."

"See?" Shay says to Jessica. "People *do* get what they deserve."

I stand behind Keisha, but I wish I could see her face. I wait for her to say something back. But Keisha doesn't say anything. Although I can't see her cry, I hear her sniff and see her brush her cheek with her fingertips.

And I watch a mind movie of me being the only girl without flowers marching in to see all the parents. And the look on my mom's face. How she'd be the only sad parent in a sea of smiling ones. And how I'd feel like I was less than everyone else.

No one should ever feel like that.

I feel my fingertips dig into the center of my bouquet to separate the thick stems. It takes some twisting to work half the flowers out of the fancy ribbon, but I put some muscle into it. Stems crack and leaves and petals fall, spinning in the air. Landing all around my shiny new shoes.

Mrs. Muldoon has turned around to stare. Her mouth is open wide enough for a bird to build a nest in.

I hold her gaze as I hand half the flowers to Keisha. "Well, she can have some of *mine*, then."

In the end, neither of us had flowers when we walked into the auditorium.

But we had bigger smiles than anyone else.

CHAPTER 14

Boxed In
and Boxed Out

"Okay, my Fantasticos! As you know, today is Fantastico Friday, and we are going to end our day with a challenge. I'm going to break you up into groups. Each group will be given a shoe box wrapped in elastic bands—which you will not remove—with a mystery object inside. Your job is to guess what the mystery object is.

"You can do anything to the box to figure it out except open it. There are four numbered boxes that will rotate from group to group. You have ten minutes with each box, so be sure that you write down your guesses. At the end, we'll open them up to see what each object is." He claps once, loudly. "Any questions?"

Everyone looks excited. Most glance around the room, probably hoping they will be with Albert. He'll get every answer right.

But I end up in a group with Max, Suki, Oliver, and Jessica. I briefly consider going to the nurse. Especially when I have to stare at all of Jessica's friendship bracelets. I wonder if each bracelet is from a different friend. I glance down at my empty wrist.

Box number one is dropped on our table. Oliver grabs it and shakes it hard. Jessica folds her arms and rolls her eyes—her response to anything not done or said by Shay. I look across the room. Shay is in a group with Albert. She's holding the box and talking. What a surprise.

"Yeah," Max says, taking the box from Oliver. "My turn."

I'm surprised when Suki speaks up first. "Oliver. We all need a turn, so we must plan. Ten minutes and five of us. Two minutes each."

I think about the nurse again. I could lie on that comfortable bed and think. I've come up with some of my best sketchbook ideas pretending to be sick down there.

Max has been shaking the box. He throws it into the air once and catches it. "Whatever's inside is heavy," he says.

Oliver says, "Maybe it's a kangaroo."

Jessica looks at him in disgust.

Oliver shrinks. "I was just kidding," he mumbles.

This makes me mad.

Max hands it to Jessica, who gives it a little shake and says, "I think it's a wooden block. Like maybe one of those alphabet blocks."

"When will it be my turn again?" Oliver asks.

Suki is taking some kind of notes or something. Looking up at the clock, she says, "Oliver, you have twenty-five seconds of your time left only."

Oliver takes the box back and sniffs it and tries to hear something by pressing his ear to the top.

Mr. Daniels calls from the other side of the room, "I love that, Oliver. Creative investigation!"

While I wait for my turn, I wonder why Oliver always smells like graham crackers. Finally, I get the box and put it up to my ear and tilt it. Whatever is inside rolls rather than slides. "It must be round. And Max is right about it being heavy."

I tilt it again with my palm on the side of the box. "I think it's a baseball," I say, handing it to Jessica.

She does the same test and surprises me by saying, "I agree. Feels like a baseball."

"Wait," I say, taking it back. I tilt it again quickly and the object hits the end hard, and then lightly. "It bounces," I say. "Would a baseball bounce?" I ask, turning to Max.

"Naw. I don't think so. Maybe it's rubber. Like a lacrosse ball."

After Suki tests the box, she writes down our answer.

Then we get the second box. The second item slides rather than rolls. I can tell because it doesn't move if the box is tilted a little but, once tilted more, will move all at once. And I can feel it scraping along the bottom. It's weird, but I can almost see it. It's heavier than an alphabet block, but I think it is a shape with all flat sides.

Oliver tells me that it's cool I'm so good at this. I forget to say thank you because I'm shocked. But then I also forget to be nervous, talking to everyone and feeling like . . . like I can do this as well as everyone else, and it is the *best*. The best feeling ever.

Suki hands the box to me. "Your turn to go first."

The third box is harder, but I guess it's in the shape of a Magic Marker but much bigger and heavier, as it slides one way and rolls the other.

I glance over at Albert, who is listening to Shay talk again. Keisha is doing the talking in her group, but she is making everyone laugh. I wish I knew what they were saying.

When Mr. Daniels delivers the fourth box, he stays.

While Max tries to figure out what's inside, Jessica constantly compliments him on everything short of breathing. Max tells us that he thinks it's something light because it doesn't hit the sides hard.

When it is his turn, Oliver looks up at Mr. Daniels.

"So, what do you think there, Oliver?"

I can see Oliver wants to be right. He tilts and shakes and decides it's a quarter. Mr. Daniels nods and pats him on the back. "That's an excellent guess, Oliver. Well done."

"Am I right?" Oliver asks.

"You'll have to wait and see." Mr. Daniels shrugs.

"Can't you just tell me now?"

"Sorry, bud."

Oliver seems disappointed. Then he looks up at me. Holding out the box, he says, "Here, Ally. You're the best at this."

Jessica's face looks like if she let out all that pressure, she'd fly into the air like a rocket to the moon.

"Ally?" Mr. Daniels asks.

"Huh? Uh, sorry. Sometimes when I think, I forget to talk."

He laughs a little.

I hold the box in front of me with the long side almost touching my stomach. I tilt the box front to back and then side to side. This doesn't make sense.

"What are you thinking, Ally?" he asks.

"Well," I begin, "if I tilt it front to back, the object hits the long sides of the shoe box. But if I tilt it side to side, the object doesn't hit the short sides."

In my mind, I see the object must be the size and shape of a magic wand. Because it moves a lot when tilted in one direction but not when tilted in the other.

"What?" Oliver asks.

"It doesn't make sense," I say. I look down at the box and shake it side to side hard. I can't get the object to hit the sides of the box. The more I shake side to side, the more it hits the top and bottom of the box. Confusing.

I look up at Mr. Daniels and his half smile and scrunched eyebrows.

"Waaaait a second." I smile. "Would you trick us?"

"What do you mean, trick you?"

I shake it again. Tilt it some more. "The object hits some sides but not all sides. Did you tape it or tie it or something?"

His eyes widen quick and he smiles. And then he laughs. He laughs loud, bending over and resting his hands on his knees, and then he swings his head to the side to look over at me. By this time, the whole class is watching him.

"Wow, Ally Nickerson. That's amazing. I have done this with over a hundred kids and no one—in all of those times—has ever been able to figure that out."

He reaches over and takes the box. Taking the elastic bands off, he opens the box to show us all what's inside. It's two glue sticks tied together with string, and then the ends of the string are taped to the sides of the box, leaving the glue sticks hanging in the middle.

He comes over and does something a teacher has never done even once in my whole life. He high-fives me.

CHAPTER 15

Ungreased Gears

For homework, Mr. Daniels said we have to write a paper describing how we feel about a short story he read today. He says there's no right or wrong answer. He just wants to know our thoughts.

Part of my brain knows that this shouldn't be that hard. I would be able to tell him in two minutes how I feel about it. But I'll be celebrating another birthday by the time I get it written down. And when I do, he probably won't be able to understand it anyway.

Travis comes in the back door, drops his bag, and takes off his steel-toed boots. "Hey, squirt." The smell of a garage fills the kitchen. But I like it.

"Hey," I say, trying to get the thoughts floating around in my head to land on the paper. I don't know why the things in my brain get lost on the way down my arm.

Travis takes a carton of orange juice out of the fridge and drinks from it.

"*Hello*, Travis? *Gross.*"

He laughs at me.

"No one else will drink that now, you know."

"Good." He smiles. "My plan is a success." He walks away, taking the whole carton with him.

"Travis?"

He stops in the hallway after taking another swig. "Yeah?"

I know what his answer will be, but I ask anyway. I'm desperate. "Can you help me?"

"With that book stuff you're doing?" He points using the carton.

"Yeah. I have to write something . . ."

"Whoa, Ally. I can give you new spark plugs. Change your oil. Even rebuild your carburetor. But the writing? No can do. When it comes to that, my brain is like gears with no grease. Parts grinding together. Seriously. It ain't pretty."

"Please? You *have* to be better at it than me."

He takes a deep breath. "Can't you wait until Mom gets home?"

"She left a message saying she's closing, and I can't tell her I need help that late. She'll be mad."

"Look. You know I'd love to help you out, but the whole school thing . . . It's like asking a blind man to drive a bus. Besides," he says, sipping again, "I'd rather eat a bag of hair."

He's trying to make me laugh and the picture in my head is funny. And kind of gross. But I can't laugh. I can't. I'm too desperate.

I must look sad because his voice is sweet. "Seriously, Al. I would help you, but I'm no better at it than you. I'm really not."

The next morning, I am trying to decide if I should turn in my paper, knowing Mr. Daniels will probably think I spit it out in two minutes. The truth is that it cost me my whole night and a headache that was so bad, it reminded me of the Queen in *Alice in Wonderland* always yelling, "Off with her head!" Just because I thought that would be a relief.

I worry what Mr. Daniels will say about it. For now, he's in the hallway with another kid.

"Good morning," Keisha says. "I have something for you." And she holds out a cupcake.

"Cupcake!" Max says.

"Put your eyes back in your head, Max. This is not for you," Keisha says.

"Me want cupcake!" Oliver says, flailing about a bit. "Me *love* cupcakes!"

"You're such a freak," Shay says. "That's Cookie Monster who talks like that."

Oliver gets dead serious. Not a single thing on him is moving except his mouth. "If I'm talking like that, then *I'm* the one talking like that. And besides, do you *really* think that Cookie Monster would turn down a cupcake? I mean, it isn't broccoli or nuclear sludge or something. You could tell him it's a big, tall cookie with frosting on it. He'd suck it down like a vacuum cleaner. I bet you he would. You want to bet me? *Do* you?"

Jessica begins to speak, but Shay cuts her off with a look. "No. I won't bet you. I don't bet on anything. Ever. And especially not with you."

Shay spins on her foot and leaves. Jessica scurries after her.

It takes three quarters of a second for Oliver to be onto something else. "Wait! That reminds me," he says. "During our class party, I hid a Halloween cookie somewhere in my desk."

"The *Halloween* party?" Keisha asks. "That was *weeks* ago."

"Yeah!" He starts digging for it, things falling to the floor as he searches. If it's there, it's probably as hard as concrete.

Keisha turns back to me. "What is it with this class? They lose control over food." She shakes her head and then pushes the cupcake toward me. "For *you*!"

"For me?" I ask. Nobody ever brings me anything. Except trouble.

"Yeah! Of course it's for you!"

"Why?"

"Because I'm still cracking up over what you did with those flowers, that's why." She cuts the cupcake in half and shows me that it says *Wow* inside.

I'm happy.

Mr. Daniels walks back into the room. "Okay, my Fantasticos! Good news! All homework assignments have been passed in today. That's worth five extra minutes of snack time."

The boys are as excited as if they've heard there would be free pizza delivered, too.

I hear Keisha kind of laughing to herself. I figure it's because of the boys all going nuts. But then she turns to me and says, "You've got guts, Ally. I respect that."

I like that, too. But mostly I like that she likes it.

"Hey," she says. "You want to sit together at lunch? I've been sitting with some people, but I don't talk to them and they don't talk to me. And you sit alone, so . . ."

A mind movie shows us sitting at the table talking and me being happy.

"Ally? What do you think?"

"Oh! Yes, that would be great. Thank you."

After the best lunch and recess I've had in a long time, Mr. Daniels waves me up to his desk. He has my homework and my journal. He's trying to look all happy and light, but I can see the seriousness underneath.

"Hey, Ally. I'm glad you turned in your homework and it's more than you usually write. That's great."

I stay quiet.

"I'm just wondering how long it took you to do your homework. I'm not going to ask you to make changes or anything. I'm just wondering."

This feels like a trap. I know it isn't good, so I wonder if it would be better to say I did it fast on the bus or if I should tell him that I worked really hard.

"Ally?"

"It took me . . . kind of a long time, I guess. I mean, I tried to do my best on it." I look at it. "Is it wrong?"

"It's got some good ideas and that's what the assignment was all about. No worries, okay?"

No worries? That's easy for him to say.

CHAPTER 16

What I've Got

I like Mr. Daniels, but he's got a thing for reading. Always talking about books and how great they are. Personally, I'd rather have the flu.

The last thing Mr. Daniels said yesterday was that we were going to write stories today and that it would be our chance to show him what we've got.

The only thing I've got is a plan.

With a big piece of cloth and a safety pin, my writing arm hangs in a sling. How can he ask me to write like this? I'm feeling pretty proud, I must admit. All I have to do is remember not to move it. I wish it really did hurt; it would be easier.

He sees me when I walk in and it isn't long before he

comes over to ask me what has happened. I have practiced the story all the way to school. About how I tripped over my cat on the stairs and fell.

"You have a cat?" he asks.

"Yeah."

He nods. Then he glances down at my sling. "Is it a new cat?"

"No, we've had that cat forever. A regular member of the family," I say, feeling like I'm starring in a commercial for something I'd never eat in a million years.

He has a weird look on his face when he asks, "What's its name?"

"Whose name?"

"Your *cat*."

I panic. "Pork Chop" pops out of my mouth.

He laughs. "Pork Chop the cat, huh? I bet the dogs in the neighborhood like that."

I'm nervous and embarrassed. Wondering why I have to be so weird. Wondering why I now have to watch the mind movie in my head of a furry, meowing pork chop with a tail.

But when the rest of the class sits down to do their writing assignments, he says I can read a book. I stare at the letters and watch them dance and move on the bright white page. My eyes ache and my head hurts.

Mr. Daniels watches me, so I look down at the page

and remember to turn it every once in a while. With my eyes closed, I watch bright movies of me flying—one of my favorite movies. In this one, I'm flying just above the water—my stomach almost touching it. Racing toward a castle filled with blue light.

I open my eyes a bit to watch the others write. I look at the page again. I even try to read some. I really do. But I can't help wondering why Mr. Daniels keeps looking over at me.

CHAPTER 17

Misfit Lunch

I watch Albert sit at his desk and stare at the pages of a book. I know he's not reading. His eyes don't move at all. I see he has a new bruise on his jaw and decide I'll go over and talk to him.

"Hey," I say.

He looks up.

Then something comes out of my mouth that I don't expect. "Do you want to sit with Keisha and me at lunch?"

"Why?"

"Well, you sit alone and we sit alone—but together, too—so I thought that we could all sit alone together."

"That isn't a logical conclusion. Clearly, if we are all together—"

"Yeah," I interrupt. "I know. It was a joke. So, you want to?"

"Well . . . I suppose so. I guess I've got to eat some-where," he says.

Albert leans his chair back as he shakes his empty carton of chocolate milk to let the drops fall on his tongue. "I wonder who decided that a half pint of milk was enough."

"Why don't you just buy two?"

He puts his chair down and stares.

"Can't you just ask your mom for extra money in the morning?" I say, readjusting my fake sling. This thing is a pain.

"I don't have to ask for money. It's kind of prepaid."

And then I realize all at once. Of course. How stupid can I possibly be? Albert doesn't have many clothes and he gets a ticket from Mr. Daniels every morning. I guess I never thought about it before. He must get one of the free lunches. I hope I didn't upset him, so I say, "I'm sorry."

"About what?"

"Well, about . . . well, you know. That you get the free lunch."

He shrugs. "There are worse things. Than a free lunch, I mean."

"Yeah, I guess."

"It disturbs my mom, but my dad says he wants to leave his mark on mankind with one of his inventions, and she says he should get a real job. They fight about it a lot, actually."

I'm really surprised he told me that and I decide to never tell another soul about it.

"Hey," says Keisha, sitting down.

"Hey," I say, and Albert nods.

"So, Albert," Keisha says. "I watched *Star Trek* because you are always spouting off about it. The special effects are not that special. Kind of pathetic, actually. Like a first-grade puppet show."

Albert looks horrified.

Keisha laughs as she unwraps her sandwich. "Yeah, I knew that would getcha."

Shay's voice arrives before she does. "Look, Jessica," she says as they walk by. "It's the Island of Misfit Toys."

"Yeah," Jessica says. "It's like a six-legged freak."

Shay laughs and Jessica looks proud of herself.

"Uh, those girls are like walking pricker bushes," Keisha says, taking a bite of her sandwich. "Don't let them bother you."

"They don't bother me," Albert says.

"It doesn't bother you at *all* that she called us misfit toys?" I ask.

"It doesn't bother *me*," Keisha says. "That girl can flap her gums about me until the sun rises and sets again. I really don't care."

I wish I didn't care. And I wish I wasn't jealous of Shay and all that she has.

Albert is wide-eyed. "But *why* are the toys all misfits? Square wheels on a train can be fixed easily enough." Albert has his most serious voice turned up to high. "And what's wrong with the doll, anyway? Why is it a misfit? It seems to adhere to the standards of a typical doll."

Wow. He is in full professor mode.

"The Charlie-in-the-box," he continues, "is just like a Jack-in-the-box in every way but his name. Something is not a misfit simply because it has a different name."

"That isn't true," I blurt out.

He looks shocked. I suppose he isn't used to being corrected.

He holds up his milk carton. "Suppose I say this is orange juice. Doesn't change what it is inside."

"That's different," I say, thinking that the milk will feel like it's orange juice if it's told that enough.

"It *is* the same principle."

I think of words like *dumb* and *baby* and think how wrong Albert really is.

"What about the cowboy?" Keisha asks. "He rides an ostrich instead of a horse. That has *got* to make him a misfit."

"It is illogical to say he is a misfit just because he chooses to ride a different animal, provided he can carry out his cowboy duties."

"Albert!" Keisha says. "How can you *possibly* say 'cowboy duties' with a straight face?"

"I don't understand," he says.

Keisha's forehead touches the table, and he continues, "Especially when you consider that ostriches run faster than horses, require less water to drink, and can use their legs and feet as weapons. They are fierce kickers with sharp claws. I, for one, would trade a horse for that. That's just logical."

And then I think that if someone hung a sign on me that said anything, having that sign there wouldn't make it so. But people have been calling me "slow" forever. Right in front of me as if I'm too dumb to know what they're talking about.

People act like the words "slow reader" tell them everything that's inside. Like I'm a can of soup and they can just read the list of ingredients and know everything about me. There's lots of stuff about the soup inside that they can't put on the label, like how it smells and tastes and makes you feel warm when you eat it. There's got to be more to me than just a kid who can't read well.

CHAPTER 18

Truths and Untruths

Keisha drops into her seat, annoyed that Mr. Dan-iels has asked her to do a paper over because he knows she can do better. I've always hated hearing that from teachers. And then I realize I've never heard it from Mr. Daniels. And all of a sudden that bugs me.

Since the day of the mystery boxes, I keep thinking about how good it felt to do something right. To fit in.

That's what I want. To feel like everyone else. To be told that the work I know is terrible isn't good enough. I want him to tell me I can do better and see it in his face that he really thinks so.

And then I remember that it *is* the best I can do. I haven't written in class since I had the fake sling on my arm. After three days of wearing it, Mr. Daniels told me he was going to have the nurse call my mom about my injured arm, so I figured I'd better lose the sling.

So now I'm stuck. I don't know who to be: the one who admits that I can't do it, or the pretender.

Finally I decide I'll give Mr. Daniels something so, so terrible that he'll have to ask me to do it over.

I don't even try to spell anything correctly like I usually do. I just put a whole bunch of letters together that even I know make no sense.

I walk up and hand it to him instead of putting it in the assignment cubby.

"Thanks, Ally, but if you're done, why don't you put it in the cubby?"

I push it toward him a little more. "I thought you may want to check it over."

We lock eyes for a few seconds and then he reaches out to take it from me. "Okay," he says. He looks at it, his eyebrows scrunch up, and then he looks back up at me. He stays quiet. Thinking, I can tell.

I hear it in my head. *Do better, Ally.* And I would. I would magically do better and Mrs. Silver would carry a trophy for me so big, she'd have to carry it on her back.

"Ally?"

"Huh?"

"I said that you can just put it in the cubby, then."

And the pictures in my head pop like bubbles. I walk away without taking it back.

As soon as we all sit down in the cafeteria, Keisha announces to Albert, "Okay. This has been killing me. All. Day. Long."

"What?" I ask.

"Albert. So this Flint shirt that you wear every day."

He interrupts. "I do not, in fact, wear the same shirt every day. I have five identical ones."

Keisha's eyes are wide. "Seriously, Albert? You bought the same shirt five times?"

He doesn't seem to think it's a big deal. "It's the one I liked."

"Well, anyway, Albert," Keisha says. "I finally found out what the heck your shirt means. I googled 'Flint' and you know what I found?"

His eyes widen.

"It's a place in Michigan, a kind of rock, something people use to light campfires, what arrowheads are made of, and a kind of sneaker."

Albert doesn't say anything.

"Albert? Did you *hear* me? What is with the Flint shirt? That just makes no sense . . . No sense whatsoever."

Albert fidgets.

"Hey, Albert," I say. "You okay? You know, Keisha didn't mean any harm. She just . . ."

"I am quite aware of her intentions."

I worry. "What are those?"

"To find out why I wear this shirt."

Funny how my brain wants to make things complicated and his just cuts to the simplest thing. Well, the simplest thing with a bunch of fancy words and mile-long sentences.

"The meaning of my shirt is not any of those things." He closes his eyes before he takes a deep breath. "Flint is an immortal genius from *Star Trek*. Season three, episode nineteen. It is titled 'Requiem for—'"

Keisha laughs, interrupting him. "Albert, are you *kidding* me?"

Albert clears his throat and glances at the clock.

"Albert," I say, poking the side of Keisha's leg, and she—by some miracle—stops laughing. "Go ahead. I want to know." After that day of being mean, I want to be extra nice. "So, Flint is a smart guy?" I ask.

Albert readjusts himself in his seat. "Flint goes away to his own planet. He puts up invisible barriers so that others won't sense life-forms there. He creates robots to protect himself and keep him company. They are . . . *predictable*."

"Sounds super weird if you ask me," says Keisha. "Why wouldn't he live on Earth with people?"

"He had once lived on Earth. He left to be alone. He *wanted* to be alone."

Keisha falls forward, dropping her arms on the table. "Why the heck would a man leave Earth with everything here to go off and sit on some rock in space all by himself?"

Albert hesitates. "Well . . . he says it's to 'retreat from the unpleasantness of Earth and the company of people.'" Then he looks up right into my eyes. "I can see that. I can see why someone would want to avoid being with other people. A great number of them are not very nice to me . . . and, well . . ."

"Listen, Albert." Keisha's voice has softened. "I didn't mean . . ."

Albert interrupts. "I was not implying it was you who is not kind to me."

I'm relieved.

"But there are others who are not kind," he says.

CHAPTER 19

Not-So-Sweet Secret

Just as I thought, my mother smiles when she sees Albert, Keisha, and me walk into Petersen's. She seats us in a booth right in the middle of the restaurant and takes our order. Keisha sits next to me and Albert fills a good part of the seat across from us.

"So," Keisha begins. "Thanks for inviting us for ice cream."

"You're welcome."

"Must be cool to come here every day," she says.

"Is the ice cream free?" Albert asks.

"My mom doesn't let me have ice cream more than once a week. And it isn't free, but we get it for half off, I think," I tell them.

Albert fidgets a bit. "So, do either of you ever miss Mrs. Hall?"

"Our old *teacher* Mrs. Hall?" I say. "She was okay, but I like Mr. Daniels way more. He's nice."

"He is," Keisha says. "Goofy, but in a good way."

"Yeah," I say.

"I do not think he is a trusting person," Albert says.

"Mr. *Daniels*?" I ask.

Albert rubs his palms on the top of his jeans. "He inquired about my bruises. I think he hypothesized that they came from my parents. Then I had to speak to the school psychologist." He shifts in his seat. "My parents rescue insects and arachnids from our home, taking them outside rather than killing them. It's illogical for my parents to save spiders and hit their own son."

I look over at Keisha. Hoping she knows what to say. She doesn't.

I take a deep breath. "Well, Albert, even I've wondered where all those bruises come from."

His voice is quiet. Like a boy. Not a robot version of one. "There's a group of boys. I meet them many days after school."

"You *meet* them?" Keisha asks.

"Well, no," he says. "They meet *me*."

"I'm sorry," I say.

He nods once and then stares at the floor.

"Can't you tell anyone?" I ask.

Albert shrugs.

"Well do you at least hit them *back*?" Keisha asks.

"I don't believe in violence. And anyway, it seems to me that big kids would get the blame in a fight. No one's going to think a big kid like me didn't start it, so they would assume I give the punches, not receive them."

He stares at his vanilla ice cream and then looks up. Maybe a little happier. "This reminds me of ice cream on Ellis Island."

"You may have a skull full of brains, but, *again*, Albert . . . no sense," Keisha says.

"When the immigrants came to America through Ellis Island, they would sometimes get ice cream for a treat. But they didn't recognize ice cream. They thought it was butter, so they spread it on toast."

We laugh.

"I think this is like that. Those boys just think I'm a fighter, so they . . . well, fight me."

"No, Albert," Keisha says. "They think you *won't* fight. They think you'll just keep being their punching bag. *That's* why they fight you."

His eyebrows scrunch up.

"*Albert*. This is no joke," Keisha says. "They leave nasty marks on you! Don't your parents get mad? My mother would hunt down anyone who did that to me."

"My father is busy with his inventions and my mother has other things to worry about."

"You should ask them for help," I say. "I think Keisha is right."

He shrugs. "I don't want help. I should be able to solve this."

"Albert!" Keisha says, her dark eyes wide and angry. "You *can* solve this. Just don't let those boys pound on you! You said you're bigger than they are."

"Yes, I call them the fire ants. A group of small beings that can become overwhelming."

I laugh, but I'm sad on the inside.

"No, seriously, Albert." Keisha is downright mad now. "Teach them a lesson. Hit them back!"

"I don't think it is within my nature to hit someone. I will not meet violence with violence. I won't stoop to their level."

"Stoop to their level?" I ask.

"If I act like them, I am no better," he says.

"Well, I say this is like trying to give Jell-O a spine," Keisha says.

Albert squints, which makes me wonder if he's actually mad. "Some of the most lethal creatures on earth are invertebrates."

"Don't throw that science at me," Keisha says. "All I

know is that you need to stick up for yourself. If you just let them do that, it's like telling them it's okay."

Albert stays quiet.

Keisha's voice is no longer soft. "I just don't get it, Albert. *What* in the *world* would it take for you to fight back?"

Albert looks upset. I know Keisha is trying to help him, but I think it's like throwing him an anchor for a life jacket.

"So, Albert. You've always liked science?" I ask, trying to get another conversation going. But Keisha gasps and looks at the ceiling—frustrated with Albert.

"Yes," Albert says. "But, Ally, I would like to ask *you* a question."

"Sure. Go ahead."

"Shay is not kind to many people. But I have observed that she is the most unkind to you and I don't understand it. Do you know why?"

"Yeah," Keisha says. "She really does seem to have it in for you."

"Yeah, well . . ."

"Oh, is there a story?" Keisha says. "I just love a good story."

"There's no story. I won the art award last year. She was mad about that."

"Oh no. There's more of a story, all right. Now, spill it."

"Let's just say she holds grudges."

"Spill it. Use the word *grudges* and there has got to be a really *good* story!"

"Well . . . on my second day here last year, I'd bought a bag of cheese crackers at lunch. I was assigned to sit next to her, which she wasn't so happy about. I was almost done with my sandwich when she grabbed the bag of crackers from the table and ripped them open and ate them."

"Are you kidding? She *did* that?"

I nod. I really don't want to finish this story.

"She is *unbelievable*," Keisha says, shaking her head.

"Anyway, I kind of had this habit of doing things without thinking. Well . . ." I pause. "I used to do it even more than I do now. So, when she took a piece of cake out of her lunch box, I reached over, sunk my fingernails through the frosting, grabbed a hunk, and stuffed it in my mouth."

Keisha hangs over the table laughing while Albert looks like I stuck him with a pin. "You *did* that?" he asks, wide-eyed.

"And then . . ." Uh, I really don't want to tell them this. "While I licked the frosting off of my fingers, I asked her, 'So how do you like *that*?!'"

I cringe when I think of Shay's face. Total surprise

followed by looking at me like I was a disease on two feet. And somehow, deep down inside, I knew I'd pay for that forever.

But Keisha is still laughing. "That is the *best*. More people ought to put that girl in her place. She walks all over everybody."

I kind of think out loud, "She thought I was a freak."

"She deserved it. Just taking your food like that? Are you kidding?"

"Well, the thing was," I say, and then I stop because I can't quite push out the rest. "I was mad that she'd eaten my crackers. But, when lunch was over, I reached into my jacket pocket and found mine."

Keisha laughs loud and long while Albert raises his eyebrows. "Wait," Albert says, "she didn't actually eat yours?"

I shake my head.

"So she thinks you grabbed a hunk of her cake for no reason?" Keisha asks.

"Uh, yeah. Kind of. Yeah."

Keisha's laughter gets even louder just as my mother is looking across the restaurant, giving me "the look." Keisha leans against me and says, "Okay. I admit it. That is the *best* story I've heard. In. My. Whole. Long. Life. Ally Nickerson, if I didn't love you already for that flower thing you pulled, I think I may love you for that."

CHAPTER 20

Is This a Good Thing?

I hear the front door slam and Travis calls for me. He sounds happy. I mean really happy. He appears in the doorway of my room. "Guess what?"

"What?" I ask, but he doesn't answer. He just stands there with a big, dumb grin on his face. And then I notice what he has in his hand and I jump up. "You *got* it? *Really?*"

He still doesn't answer. He just shakes the keys like a baby rattle.

So we run outside, and sitting there at the curb is a surprise. But not the kind of surprise I'd hoped for.

"I know it doesn't look like much."

But he's wrong. It looks like a lot. It's enormous and

bright green. I mean seriously. It's like a pickle with tires. "No," I say. "It's cool."

"You can't lie to me, squirt. I know you too well."

"Why are there lines on it?" I ask, leaning in.

"Oh, well, I guess the guy that had the car painted it with a brush instead of a spray gun. I'll have to sand that out. And strip the chrome on the side. But the engine is good. It's gonna fly."

The only way this thing is going to fly is if he straps it to a giant balloon. A sketchbook picture is already drawing itself in my head.

"And there are no computers in a car this old. Just a man and his machine."

I look up. "Is that really a good thing?"

He shoves me a little. "You'll love it when it can take us places. To the beach? Six Flags?"

I look up quick. "Really?"

"Wherever you want to go, squirt."

I had never imagined that his car would be *our* car. That he would take me places.

"You want to take it out with me now?"

"Sure. Am I pushing or pulling?"

"You're going to be sorry you dissed this beauty. I'm telling you. You've got to be loyal to your car."

"Travis, you do know it's only a car, right?"

"Only a car?" he asks. "Only a car?" He runs to the

other side and slides in. He unlocks the door for me and I get in, too. It's a big bench seat. The Walking Liberty half dollar hangs from his rearview mirror. It makes me feel like Dad and Grandpa are with us.

When he turns on the engine, it sounds like a giant with a bad cough. We head up Farmington Avenue past St. Thomas Church.

It had been raining all morning, and now it starts again. Big drops of rain fall on the windshield like bombs. Travis says a bad word, pulls over, and grabs a silver spring and a piece of wet rope from the glove compartment.

"What are you doing?"

He jumps out into the rain, grabbing the windshield wiper on my side and connecting it to something at the bottom of the window with the spring. Then he ties that wiper to the second wiper and throws the rope through his window and jumps in. Laughing and dripping wet.

"What the heck are you doing?" I ask.

"Three. *Hours*," he says.

"What are you talking about?"

"Three hours after this thing was registered this morning, the wiper motor went. So I went by the hardware store and rigged this up. Watch." With his left arm, he pulls the rope and the wipers clear the window of water. When he lets go, the spring yanks them back down, slapping the bottom of the window.

"Hey, I thought you said you were a genius," I joke.

"I am. All geniuses deal with bugs in the system."

"Isn't that more like what anteaters do?"

"Hilarious." He laughs.

"Isn't it a little hard to drive and do that?"

"You're right, squirt. You can do the wipers," he says, throwing the rope into the backseat. "Climb over and sit behind me."

"Okay!" I say, climbing over the seat. I give the rope a pull and then let it go, and the wipers slap up and down. It's kind of fun to see the wiper clear the window—make the blurry clear. And I think about what a great drawing this will be later and I'm happy for the weird pickle-colored car.

"Wow, this is fun—and hard," I tell Travis. My arm is getting tired.

He watches me in the rearview mirror and laughs. I laugh, too, and it makes pulling the rope even harder.

We pull up to a red light and Travis tells me to look at the face of the lady riding the car next to us, and I do. She looks shocked and I think her expression is the funniest thing I've ever seen.

Until I see Shay sitting next to her.

As soon as Mr. Daniels steps into the hallway to talk to another teacher, Shay says in her I'm-being-loud-on-purpose-so-everyone-can-hear-me voice, "So, Jessica. Yesterday,

I saw that Ally riding in this disgusting green-colored car that I can't believe was even allowed on the road. Ally had to pull a rope to even get the windshield wipers to work."

"You *must* be joking," says Jessica.

"Ally? What junkyard did you find that heap in?" Jessica laughs like she's supposed to.

I try to ignore them. My mom has always said you just ignore mean people because they are only trying to get a rise out of you.

"I mean, what kind of loser would have a car like that? Probably the only thing your mother can afford."

Finally I can't take it. "It's my brother Travis's car. And it is *not* a loser car."

"Oh no. It's a loser car all right. I guess that makes your brother Travis a loser."

They laugh.

"I didn't think there could be a bigger loser than you, Ally, but I guess I was wrong," Shay says.

"Shut up!" I say to Shay just as Mr. Daniels walks back in. "You're the losers. *You.* Not *him.*"

"Ally?" Mr. Daniels calls. "Come here, please."

"*What?*" I ask, trying not to sound disrespectful.

"I haven't known you to name-call before."

"They can call me anything they want. And believe me, they do. But they can't say anything about Travis. Never."

"Is Travis your older brother?"

"He's my *big* brother."

He half smiles. "Is there a difference?"

"Yeah. There is. An older brother is older. A big brother looks out for you and smiles when you walk into a room."

He nods slowly. "I see." He clears his throat. "I understand you're upset and I appreciate that you're defending your brother, but walk away next time. Okay?"

I nod, but I have to admit that I'm getting awfully tired of walking away.

CHAPTER 21

Butterfly Wishes

Our classroom is brainstorming ideas for a com-munity service project.

Shay raises her hand. "I am having a birthday party and inviting everyone because I don't want to leave anyone out."

"How does that relate to our community service project?" Keisha asks, and the whole class waits for an answer.

"Well, it's about community. Everyone being involved."

"Yeah, right," Keisha whispers to me.

Mr. Daniels compliments Shay on inviting everyone and moves on quickly. Later, as we get our stuff for lunch and recess, Shay speaks to Jessica in her loud voice. "I'm so mad my mother is making me invite everyone." Then she looks directly at Keisha and me and says, "I hope some people know better than to actually show up."

My mom insists I go to Shay's party. Even after I tell her that Shay is mean, my mom asks, "Well, there will be other kids there, right? You may actually have fun."

Albert grabbed his invitation from the mailbox before his mother saw it. Keisha's family is visiting her grandmother. So I'm alone.

At lunch, I ask Albert and Keisha about some diseases I can use as an excuse not to go.

"How about bubonic plague? Otherwise known as the black plague?" Albert asks.

Keisha almost spits out her milk. "*Seriously?*"

"Uh, that may be a bit much," I say, but then I begin to wonder. "What does that look like, anyway?"

"Oh, well . . . chills, fever, cramps. Seizures. Toes, fingers, nose, and lips turn black because the cells die. And you'd likely spit blood."

"*Albert,*" Keisha says. "That's nuts. She can be sick like a normal person, you know. Cough. Runny nose. Sound familiar?"

"That's fine," he says, taking a bite of his sandwich. "It just seems uninteresting, that's all."

• • •

Shay's party is at the Butterfly Gardens, and when I arrive, I recognize some girls from other classrooms. They are all wearing friendship bracelets. Jessica wears even more now. I still ache to have some and wonder if Keisha would like a bracelet like that.

Soon, we are lined up and brought to the main butterfly garden, which is a clear plastic tent set up inside a bigger room. The tent is filled with plants and flowers, and flying around are tons of butterflies. People stand there as the butterflies land on them, and you can feel how happy people are just by watching their eyes.

Before we enter the tent, a lady talks to us about the butterflies. She tells us about their patterns and to look for ones with a giant dot on each wing. These are adaptations to scare other animals into thinking they are eyes, so other animals will think they are bigger and more dangerous and leave them alone. I wish I could do this with Shay—and that Albert could do that with those boys.

She reminds us not to grab any butterflies, because they are injured easily. We are supposed to stand and let them come to us. Then the lady points to me and says, "They'll love your orange shirt."

She's right. The butterflies do come to me. Their colors and patterns make me wonder why I haven't been drawing butterflies. They don't fly like birds. Instead, they kind of fly all over the place. Makes me wonder if I'm part butterfly.

I put my arms out like a tree and one, then two land on my arm. I love them. I never knew before how much I love butterflies.

I think about the story Albert told in social studies when we were studying Native Americans. He said that they believed butterflies were special creatures and wish givers. And that if you can catch a butterfly, whisper your deepest wish to it, and then set it free, it will carry your wish to the spirits, who will grant it.

I would never grab a butterfly, but once again, my hands do things without my say-so. When a beautiful, bright orange-and-black one lands on my hand, I loosely close my fist around it.

And then my thinking part steps forward and quickly realizes what I've done. I open my hand and the butterfly zigs and zags before landing on the ground.

The lady who gave us the directions is next to me in a second. "Oh no, what have you done?" she asks.

I want to explain about wish givers, but Shay and the others appear. "It figures it was Ally. She probably killed it. Everyone knows you can't touch a butterfly's wings."

"I didn't kill it. I mean, I would never hurt it. I had a wish and I thought that . . ."

The girls laugh. "Such a freak show," Shay says.

Suki rushes to the butterfly to try and help, but a woman runs over and tells her to step back.

"Who are you with?" the woman asks me.

Shay's mother steps forward. "She's with us, but she's not my daughter. She's part of my daughter's party."

I wish my own mom were here; she'd understand. I feel terrible watching the butterfly on the ground, flapping its wings and not going anywhere. I know the feeling.

The first butterfly lady wears white gloves as she puts the injured one in a box, saying, "At least its wings aren't torn." The second lady stares at me like I'm a ruthless butterfly hunter.

I want to say I'm sorry, but I forget to because I'm watching mind movies of the butterfly falling and falling and never being better. And then the movie is filled with butterflies that are all falling like rain. And I feel as sad as I did watching the real one fall.

Suki comes over. "I know you didn't hurt the butterfly on purpose."

"Thanks," I mumble. She's right, but it was still my hand.

I guess I just had to make that wish.

Sometimes a person will do just about anything for a wish to come true.

CHAPTER 22

No Way to Treat a Queen

Later, I try to call Albert, but a recording says that the number is no longer in service, and I worry that he had to move away or something.

When I see him at school on Monday, I am so relieved.

I run up to him. "Albert, is it true that if you touch a butterfly's wings, you keep it from flying ever again? Basically, kill it?"

"A rather curious question for such a cold day. In temperatures such as these—"

"Albert! Just *tell* me. *Yes* or *no*."

"No, it is a myth that you render a butterfly unable to fly by touching its wings. The powdery residue on their wings is actually scales. They shed these scales on a regular basis, so merely touching them is okay. You only injure the butterfly if its wings are torn."

I remember how the lady said its wings weren't torn. I hug Albert until I realize what I'm doing. His surprised expression is so hilarious. Like Einstein himself just told him that Earth is not round but instead shaped like a spoon.

"Nice shirt, Albert. Is it new?" Shay laughs at her own comment. Before he can answer, she draws her fingers down her own sleeve. "I got a new sweater. It's purple, which is the color of royalty," she says, looking directly at me. "That's why it's my favorite."

I wonder what she wants from us and I hate that I never know what to say to her. I come up with great comebacks to her the next morning, hunched over a bowl of cereal.

"Indeed. Purple is the color of royalty," Albert tells Shay.

"Yes. Yes, it is." Her voice is singsongy and makes me wish she'd go eat paste.

"You two are just so uncouth." She turns to me. "I bet Ally doesn't even know what the word *uncouth* even means. *Do* you?"

"I know what *uncouth* means," Albert says. "I know

something else, too. Only an uncouth person would wear snail snot."

She looks at us like we're wearing it.

"You say purple is the color of royals," he says. "They only wore purple because it was the most difficult and expensive color to make. In medieval times, they needed to collect three thousand *Murex brandaris* snails to have enough slime to make one cloak. So, good for you. I'd prefer beige." He turns to me. "What about you, Ally? Slime or beige?"

"Oh, I'd have to go for beige." I try not to smile, as much as I want to, and I try to keep my voice from sounding as happy as it is, because the look on Shay's face when she looks down at her new sweater, like she is actually covered in snail slime, is pretty unforgettable.

CHAPTER 23

Words That Breathe

Monday is vocabulary day, when Mr. Daniels goes over the new words for the week. As far as reading lessons go, this isn't so bad. All I have to do is listen as he tells us the word's meaning, and I can usually remember it because I make mind movies about each one and that helps me remember.

I've always had one important rule in the classroom, which is to try to lie low. If I'm called upon, I'll say, "I don't know," even if I do. I discovered that giving a teacher an answer makes them expect more from me, and then everyone gets disappointed. If they never get an answer from me, they stop asking.

But today, during vocabulary, Mr. Daniels brings up two words: *alone* and *lonely*. He asks for volunteers to explain the difference between the two.

It's like my arm doesn't belong to me when it goes up. Mr. Daniels stops midsentence and looks at me.

"Yes, Ally?"

What have I done? I try to figure out what I should say. Maybe ask to go get a drink? But the thing is that something deep inside me really does want to answer. Because I'm an expert on these two words. I know what they mean. And how they feel. Especially after that butterfly party.

Mr. Daniels's eyes are wide, and they are waiting for me. "Ally?" he says. "It's okay, now. Take your time."

And it's like he can see right into my guts. Knows how sad I am. Like he's handing me a flashlight in a dark room.

I lock eyes with Mr. Daniels and I forget anyone else is even there. I say, "Well . . . *alone* is a way to be. It's being by yourself with no one else around. And it can be good or bad. And it can be a choice. When my mom and brother are both working, I'm alone, but I don't mind it." I swallow hard. Shift in my seat. "But being *lonely* is never a choice. It's not about who is with you or not. You can feel lonely when you're alone, but the worst kind of lonely is when you're in a room full of people, but you're still alone. Or you feel like you are, anyway."

I look at Mr. Daniels. He has his hands stuffed in his pockets and his face looks sad. I try to remember what I just said, but speaking in class has made me so nervous that my mind is doing its Etch A Sketch thing. Unable to play my words back. What did I say? Why does he look like that?

Staying quiet and having people think you're stupid is better than talking and having people know for sure.

Mr. Daniels says my name.

"Huh?"

No one laughs. Not even Shay or Jessica.

"Well," he says, "if I had a trophy to give out for the best answer of the year, I'd give it to you for that." He throws his hands up as if to celebrate. "That was . . . well, *excellent!*"

I stare at my desk, wondering why he would say that.

"Ally?"

I look up. "Thanks," I say, feeling like I have to move. Leave. Why is he acting like I won the Brain Olympics just because I answered a question? "Can I please go to the bathroom now?"

Mr. Daniels seems confused. "Uh, yeah. Sure, Ally. Go ahead."

When I stand, Shay squints at me and shakes her head. She doesn't even have to say anything and my brain plays the things she *would* say.

Even when I do something right, I feel like I've done something wrong. If I were a coin, I'd be a wooden nickel.

CHAPTER 24

Imaginary Hero

Mr. Daniels asks us to write about our favorite fictional character—a person we consider to be a hero— and be ready to tell the class about who it is. It's funny how much trouble Albert has with this. He tells Mr. Daniels that looking up to a character that isn't real is illogical, but Mr. Daniels tells him it will be good for him, which confuses the heck out of Albert. He mumbles all the way back to his seat. Albert never mumbles. He either talks or he doesn't.

Oliver is in his seat listing the names of every superhero I've ever heard of. "Superman, Captain America, Batman." He looks upset when he turns to Suki nearby. "Is Robin a superhero? I mean, his outfit isn't scary. At all.

And he has no special powers. But Batman doesn't really, either. But at least Batman can drive the Batmobile and fly the Batplane. Robin just rides along. I don't think I'd want to just ride along. What do you think?"

Suki opens her mouth but no sound comes out. It doesn't matter, because Oliver has moved on. "Spider-Man. Maybe I'll write about him." He holds up his palm in Suki's face. "He shoots webs. And he swings from buildings. That would be the BEST!"

"Hey, freak," Shay whispers, glancing over at Mr. Daniels, who is working with someone at his desk, to make sure he can't hear. "We don't need to hear every weird thought in your tiny little brain. We're trying to work."

Oliver's face is unmoving. Until he says, "If. I. Were. Aquaman. I. Would. Summon. The *piranhas*. To take you away. You could be their queen."

Keisha starts laughing and Mr. Daniels finally looks up. "Keisha?"

She puts her arm down on her desk and leans her forehead against it. Trying to stop laughing. The more she tries, the more Shay glares. With Mr. Daniels watching, most everyone goes back to their work. After a while, even Keisha does.

But I keep looking around the room. I love how Albert can't choose one character while Oliver wants to write about everyone.

However, I don't love how much trouble I'm having writing about my character. Makes me wish that *I* were a fictional character.

When Mr. Daniels calls me up to his desk, he's holding my paper. A teacher holding my paper is rarely a good thing. But Mr. Daniels doesn't cover my papers with red ink like other teachers. They used to look like they were bleeding.

Mr. Daniels has written in green and he apologizes for not being able to read my writing. He says that my character sounds really interesting, but he'd like to know a bit more. "Will you read this out loud for me?"

Uh-oh. I take it, squeezing my eyes into slits. Trying to read my own writing. I wait for him to pressure me to try harder. To do something I can't do.

He slides the paper out of my hand. "Well," he says, "why don't you just tell me instead of reading? First of all, tell me your person's name."

I feel such relief that I'm afraid to blink. I hate this pressure. But this time I've been saved. I keep my voice down so no one can hear. "It's Roy G. Biv."

"Oh, wait," he says. "Like the colors of the color spectrum?"

I nod.

He stares. Before he can tell me I've messed up the directions, I say, "You said fictional, and I figured you meant a book character like Alice from *Alice in Wonderland*, but Roy isn't real and there isn't any other character that means as much to me as him. I love the colors and I use them in my art and art is about the only thing . . ." I stop before I confess to feeling like a failure at everything else.

"That's clever, Ally," he tells me. "I actually like that you chose someone who isn't a book character, exactly. You think out of the box."

I see a mind movie of me standing outside a huge glass box. Everyone else is inside it. Together.

"Do you know what it means to think out of the box?" he asks.

I shake my head.

"It means that you are a creative thinker. You think differently than other people."

Great. Just once, I want to be told I'm like everyone else.

"It's a good thing to be an out-of-the-box thinker. People like that are world-changers."

Wait. His face doesn't look like this is a bad thing. "Is that like setting the world on fire?" I ask, smiling a bit.

"Exactly that." He nods.

Then he stares at me long enough for me to wonder what he's thinking before sending me back to my seat.

The next day, when it's time to tell the class who my character is, I begin by asking everyone what their favorite color is. It's fun. I think this part of being a teacher would be cool. I'd rather eat crayons than do the rest of it, though.

I take out a color wheel that I made at home. It's white cardboard and I've broken it into seven pie-shaped pieces. I figured out that each angle has to be about 51 degrees to have seven equal pie pieces. I used Travis's protractor to draw the lines exactly. Then I colored each piece with a different Roy G. Biv color and I made them really dark. "What color do you get if you mix all the colors together?" I ask. Most kids guess dark colors.

"My favorite color is white," I say, "because it is a mixture of all the colors."

Albert nods a little.

Shay tells everyone that it makes no sense, but I know the answer.

"If you mix paint together, that's true, but if you're talking about just the colors, pure in nature, they make white when mixed together. I brought this wheel to prove it." I feel like a magician. I show them the wheel with all its colors. Then I stick a paper clip that I've unbent through a hole in the center and spin the wheel. It turns white as it spins fast. As it slows down, the colors reappear.

Jessica leans forward. "That's pretty cool."

Shay looks at her with squinty eyes until Max agrees. Then she nods and agrees, too.

"Are you going to give that away?" Oliver asks.

I hesitate. "I wasn't going to . . ." I look down at it. "But I guess I could."

"You like that, huh, Oliver?" Mr. Daniels asks.

"I'd give it to my bus driver. She likes things with rainbow colors."

"Well, that's thoughtful of you, Oliver!" Mr. Daniels says.

I sit down at my desk, thinking about whether I should give the colored disc to Oliver. Jessica and Shay are talking behind me.

"Can I have another bracelet?" Jessica asks Shay.

"I don't think so. I can hardly keep up with people wanting them. Besides, you already have enough."

"Well, I wouldn't mind another."

There is a pause and I want to turn around. But I'm not supposed to be listening in.

"*Listen,*" Shay says. "You have seven already. I have other orders to fill first. And besides that, you still owe me three dollars for the last one. I'm not giving you another until you pay me for what's already on your wrist."

Wait. I whip around. I can't help it. "You *charge* your friends for those friendship bracelets?"

"Eavesdrop much? Yeah, so what? You want one?"

Jessica leans forward. "Wait. You're going to give *her* one?"

"No, idiot. I'm not going to *give* her one. She's going

to pay me. But you know what? Ally should pay more. A lot more." She turns to me. "Ten dollars."

I laugh. "Uh, no, thanks. I'd rather wear handcuffs."

I can't believe Shay charges her friends for something that's supposed to stand for loyalty and friendship. And I can't believe they paid.

"You are *such* a dope, Ally Nickerson," Shay says.

I look over at Keisha and Albert and realize that I have been. I've been lucky all along but didn't see it.

CHAPTER 25

Celebration or Devastation?

Mr. Daniels is wearing a tie with little trophies on it. Also, he has a goofy smile on his face. Even goofier than most days.

"Okay, my Fantasticos! There is one among you who is even more fantastic than usual—and that's hard to do. So, we are going to celebrate. You see, when you all wrote those nature poems the other day, you had all been secretly entered in"—he puts his arms up and raises his voice—"the first annual Fantastico Poetry Award."

Oh, great. Another thing for Shay to brag about. I look over at Albert and hope he will win instead. He's hoping so, too. I can tell by how he pulls his chair in more, like he's getting ready. I think that Suki has a good shot as well.

"So," Mr. Daniels begins, "this poem is a splendid surprise. Great work. And I am very happy to give the first annual Fantastico Poetry Award to . . ."

I watch Shay out of the corner of my eye. If she wins, we'll never hear the end of it.

What she does doesn't make sense. She shows surprise, but it's followed by disgust.

Mr. Daniels's hand on my shoulder makes me jump.

"Congratulations, Ally," Mr. Daniels says.

This can't be. It's too early for April Fool's Day. I look over at Albert and Keisha, wondering if they put a poem in with my name.

Mr. Daniels takes a step back and says, "C'mon. Come claim your prize."

Prize? I swallow hard.

Mr. Daniels stands at the front of the room, waving me up. "Well, what are you waiting for?"

I stand and walk toward him like the floor will swallow me up. I turn toward the class and he puts his hand on my shoulder.

He holds the poem in his hand. I look and see it is actually mine. Maybe I was just having a good day. I mean, it's about time I have a good day for once, right?

Happiness seeps in. Have I really won an award?

The thought of that would have been something for my Sketchbook of Impossible Things before now.

Me.

"So, Ally is our first poetry winner for her piece entitled, 'Rain, Rain.'" He turns to me. "Do you want to read it, or shall I?"

The paper crinkles in my hand. "I'll read it," I say, happy that I have it memorized.

> *"Rain, rain falling down*
> *Down, down on the ground*
> *All the birds go in the trees*
> *They don't like the rain, you see."*

It doesn't take long to say, but it took me a long time to write. But now it's all worth it.

There is silence until Mr. Daniels motions to everyone to applaud. Albert and Keisha clap loudest. Mr. Daniels motions again and the applause gets louder. Oliver slaps his desk until Mr. Daniels's pulling on his ear calms him down.

Looking out over the class, I remember some of the other poems I heard people working on. Really good poems.

And then the whole thing hits me. I finally get it.

Mr. Daniels holds out a certificate with fancy letters

and swirls around the edges. He also holds a coupon for a free ice cream in the cafeteria, and I think how happy Albert would be if I gave that to him.

But I can't reach out and take them. I look up into his face. He smiles and then he winks. I look out over my classmates, who have stopped clapping. Shay has pressed her mouth into a flat line. Most glance at each other with knowing looks. They all know but figure I don't.

This isn't a poetry award.

This is a pity award.

I look up at Mr. Daniels, who gives me a serious nod, as if to say, *Go ahead and take it. They don't know.*

Getting an award for not being smart enough to deserve it is the worst feeling I've ever felt. Like getting this certificate is going to make me pat myself on the back and, somehow, transform into a different person. I swear that I'll never accept an award that I don't deserve.

Never.

Keisha calls my name as I run from the room.

CHAPTER 26

Stalling

I run into the bathroom and hide in the stall at the end. I stand, pressing myself up against the wall. Embarrassed and humiliated and never wanting to go back.

The door opens and someone comes in.

"You okay?" Keisha asks.

"*No. I'm not.*"

"You won an award. Who in the world runs from an award? I'd think you'd be happy."

"I didn't. I didn't win for *real*."

"What are you talking about?" she asks. "Of course you did. I was there."

"No. Trust me. I didn't. He just . . . He's just trying to be nice."

"Why don't you come out of there?"

"You don't understand. Just go away."

"You're right, Ally. I don't understand. I don't know why you're mad about an award."

I feel so much worse than just mad. "Look," I say. "When you get on your bike, don't you expect it to hold you up? Not fall apart when you pedal?"

"Yeah. So what?"

"Imagine if every single time you got on your bike, you had to worry that the wheels would come off. And every time you ride, they do. But you still have to ride. Every day. And then you have to watch everyone watch you as the bike goes to pieces underneath you. With everyone thinking that it's your fault and you're the worst bike rider in the world."

"Why in the world are you talking about bikes and wheels coming off?"

"My brain," I say, leaning my forehead against the cold wall. "My brain will never do what I want it to do."

"C'mon. It's not like your brain is broken. So you're not the best speller. So what? Your brain seems fine to me."

"You don't understand what it's like to be different than everyone else."

"*Wait*. Have you noticed how different I look than everyone else in our class?"

"It's not the same."

"Look, you're my friend. The best friend I have here. If you want to say things like that and make it hard to be your friend, then . . . well, I'll just wait for you to come to your senses."

Oh.

"You're talking like a fool saying I don't understand what it's like to be different. But the thing is . . . I'm only different to the people who see with the wrong eyes. And I don't care what people like that think."

I laugh a little. "Albert says that the problem is that white people don't have enough melanin. He says that's the thing that makes human skin darker."

"Well, that boy is bonkers, but he is a smart one." She sounds happy. "Now, come on out."

I lean against the wall for a minute more because it's easier to say my next thing without seeing anyone. It comes from a place so deep inside, it's like it's coming out of the ground. "I just . . . I just want to fit in for once. I mean, I really do. Just to be the same as everyone else."

Keisha doesn't answer for a while. "Look. You don't fit in. I don't fit in. Albert doesn't fit in, either. Who says who fits in, anyway? People like Shay? That girl is just mean. Who cares what she thinks?"

The stall door is still closed, but I smile as I imagine Keisha's expression. I'm lucky to have her.

"Come on, Ally. Who wants to fit in with people like

Shay and her worse-than-awful friends? Thankfully we'll never fit in with people like that." Keisha laughs again. "One thing's for sure. We're not gonna fit in, but we're gonna stand out. All three of us. You wait and see. You're going to be a famous artist and Albert is going to cure cancer or invent talking fish or something."

"Talking fish? What would they say? 'Please don't fry me'?" I push the door open, and her face is just like I imagined. "And you're going to have a big baking business, right?"

"Maybe in my spare time. I'm also going to rule the world."

I laugh. Then swallow hard. "Thanks for being my friend, Keisha."

"Don't go thanking me for that. Thank me for this: I'm going to go tell Shay she has a spot on the back of her fancy riding jacket so we can watch her try to look. Then we can eat that ice cream that you won."

CHAPTER 27

Half-Baked Afternoon

Keisha invites Albert and me over to her house for a "surprise." When I arrive, Albert is already there and Keisha is wearing a baker's hat and apron.

"So, when do we eat?" Albert asks.

"No free ride here, Albert. We have to cook first," Keisha says, putting a cookbook on the table.

Albert seems disappointed.

"You'll be able to eat. Don't worry. And in the meantime, think of this as a science experiment. So it's two of your most favorite things, Albert."

I am pretty happy until she opens the cookbook and slides it over to me. "You're in charge."

"Of what?"

"The recipe! What do you think?"

What? Is she kidding?

"And Albert, you can be in charge of rolling the dough. Going to try cookie dough today to see if the letters cook at a similar rate to cake."

I'm freaking out over having to be in charge of the book. I'd rather be in charge of teaching cats to play hockey.

And my mind spins into *that* mind movie. When I start laughing, Keisha asks me what I'm doing. I have to shrug. Push the picture of a goalie cat with skates and a mouth guard out of my head.

"*Ally?*" Keisha pokes me.

"Yeah?"

"I asked, what's the first thing?"

Albert appears next to me. "I'd rather do the book. You want to trade, Ally? You can roll out the dough."

"Sure, Albert. If that's what you'd rather do, I don't mind switching."

Albert begins reading the ingredients while I roll out the cookie dough. It's sticky and hard to roll. Keisha points to a package of flour. "Hey, sprinkle some of that on."

I manage to get the dough rolled out, but I have my doubts about all of this. I look at the alphabet cookie cutters she uses to make letters. "What do you want me to spell?"

"Well, the letters are kind of big for cupcakes, so it can only be three-letter words. Spell whatever you want."

I spell "cow" because it's the first word I think of. Then we stand the letters up in the bottom of each cupcake mold and cover them with batter.

Once Keisha slides the first batch into the oven, Albert asks, "Can I have some milk?"

Keisha shrugs. "Sure," she says, taking a glass and filling it.

Albert gulps it all down and asks, "May I possibly have some more? We switched to water at home. I really miss milk."

She hands him the gallon. "Help yourself."

He sits with the milk and wraps his arm around it like he's protecting it.

I laugh. "You're not getting that back, Keisha, I hope you know."

"I have a question," Albert says after licking the milk from his lips. "If you spell 'cow' inside a cupcake, can a vegetarian eat it?"

"Boy," Keisha says. "You really take everything seriously, don't you?"

"Hey!" I turn to the oven. "Is it supposed to be smoking like that?"

Keisha pulls on a mitt. When she opens the door, smoke fills the kitchen. The cupcakes have oozed all over the tops of the pans and fallen on the bottom of the oven. It's a mess.

She groans. "Oh, man!"

"You should wait until the oven cools before you wipe it," Albert says.

Keisha turns to him. "Yeah. Thanks, Albert."

"You're welcome," he says, and she rolls her eyes.

She's disappointed that cookie dough will not work for letters. She and Albert figure out that the cookie dough expanded more than we thought it would and that's why it made such a mess.

But I just keep thinking that whenever I write something, it turns into a big mess.

CHAPTER 28

Deal of a Lifetime

"Ally?" Mr. Daniels calls me to him as the classroom empties for lunch.

"Yeah?" I ask, heading over.

"So, I've been thinking a lot about some of the answers you give during discussions. I love it when you share your opinions."

"Thanks," I say, wondering why he really called me up here.

"And I loved your thoughts on Roy G. Biv. I overheard you asking Suki about her grandfather and comparing him to yours. Well, Ally . . . I am impressed by you."

I shrug. What am I going to say? That he's crazy if

he thinks I have anything for brains but a pail full of grasshoppers?

"Really. You have some wonderful gifts. And your explanation of *lonely* and *alone*. That was clever."

I glance up at him but stare at my shoes by the time I answer. "That was just because I know about those words, *alone* and *lonely*, that's all. It was just an unfortunate stroke of luck."

He laughs. "An unfortunate stroke of luck, huh?"

I nod.

"I see."

Yeah.

"Ally, how many kids your age use phrases like 'unfortunate stroke of luck'?"

I feel like a fish in a wire cage rather than a tank. "Can I go to lunch now?"

"Not just yet. I'm wondering. Do you ever think one word but a different one comes out of your mouth?"

"Well, yeah, I guess."

"Does reading sometimes give you headaches?"

I nod, more nervous.

"When you look at letters, do they ever seem to move?"

I'm confused. "Of course they do."

"They do?" He is wide-eyed.

I nod but I'm not sure if I should.

He just looks me for a while, and I think I know how Keisha's cupcakes feel when she watches them in the oven.

"One more question," he says.

I shift my weight.

"Have you ever heard of a game called chess?"

"Yeah!" I say, happier. "It's from *Alice in Wonderland, Through the Looking-Glass*. My grandpa read it to me a gazillion times. It's the game that uses a checkerboard and the castle pieces, right?"

He brightens. "Yeah. That's the one. Do you know how to play?"

I shake my head.

"Do you want to learn?"

"I don't know."

"Well," he says, leaning forward and resting his elbows on his knees, "I think you'd like chess. I could show you how to play after school. You know, if you'd like."

"I'd have to stay after?"

He thinks for a second. "Well, I was thinking of starting a chess club. I thought you could come first so I could teach you to play. If it works out well, we could invite other kids. It might be fun. Something different."

It's not like I was born yesterday. I know he's up to something. Teachers don't volunteer to stay after school to play games. I kind of want to say yes because Mr. Daniels is cool and I don't think there is any reading stuff in chess. And my grandpa would have liked to know I could play. But it scares me. "Well, I don't think so. But thanks anyway."

He seems disappointed. I turn to go.

"How about if I excuse you from homework for learning how to play?"

I stop like my feet are strapped to thousand-pound blocks. Did he just say that? I turn around. "What's the catch?" I ask.

"No catch. If you stay after to learn chess for a few days, I'll excuse you from homework on the days you stay."

"Am I going to have to write a paper or something?"

"No papers. Promise."

"I just come in here and play a game and I get out of homework? No catch?"

"Well, you can't tell anyone in the class. I'll call your mom about it, though." He holds his hand out to shake. "We have a deal, then?"

"Yeah. Okay."

I can't say no to that deal. Homework is only one step above death.

I'm so happy about skipping some homework that I'll keep remembering it and being happy over and over again.

But what really gets me is that in order for Mr. Daniels to come up with this plan, he must have thought of me outside of school—when he didn't have to think of me. I bet other teachers have never let me sit in their head one second longer than they had to.

CHAPTER 29

Fish in a Tree

Albert, Keisha, and I get off the bus for our class trip to the Noah Webster House. With no written work today, I'm thinking it will be a silver dollar day.

Albert starts collecting acorns from the ground and filling his pockets. I'm tempted to ask why, but I'm afraid the answer will take an hour.

Oliver picks up acorns and whips them at the trees. Max joins in. Max hits a tree every time. Oliver, not so much. Mr. Daniels walks over and says something to make them stop.

I pick an acorn up, too, and it reminds me of a little Frenchman with a pointed chin. Perfectly shaped head and a little beret. I name him Pierre and stick him in my pocket. I decide that I'll do a drawing of him later. Maybe dancing with a lady at the Eiffel Tower. My grandpa always said he was going to take me to see it.

Albert's pockets are bulging by the time we line up to go inside. Shay is rolling her eyes at him and laughing. When Mr. Daniels looks in her direction, she stops like she has an on/off switch. When he looks away, she laughs at Albert again.

"Don't laugh at him," I say.

"Fine," she says. "I'll laugh at *you*."

"I don't care if you laugh at me."

Albert just stands there, looking a little lost.

"Albert," I whisper. "Why won't you tell them to go jump in a lake or at least to leave you alone?"

"Albert." Keisha talks to him in her you-better-listen-to-me voice. "Hunched over and silent is no way to meet the world."

Albert bends over, picking up more acorns. He looks up at us. "It isn't logical," he says. "It will only let them know it bothers me."

"So it *does* bother you?" I ask.

He stands up straight. "Well, no one likes to be insulted. But let's say that my worry about Shay is a drop of water in the ocean compared to my other worry right now."

"What's that?" I ask.

"These acorns," he says, holding one up. "This green

coloring on the side looks like moss, but I am concerned that it is actually a fungus. If this is the case, all of these trees may be in danger. I have collected samples and will do further research."

I lean in and look at the acorn. I like how Albert cares and is able to see things that other people wouldn't. But I wish Albert would care about himself as much as the scientific world.

Mr. Daniels puts us into groups. I pray that I end up in his group or with Keisha and Albert. I get part of my wish and am in a group with Albert. Mr. Daniels is with a bunch of boys, including Oliver and Max.

We get the drill about behaving, things being old, and how we're not supposed to touch them. We break into our groups and head upstairs and into a bedroom.

"So," our guide says, straightening her bonnet. "Does anyone know where the term *sleep tight* came from?"

Albert raises his hand and she calls on him with a smile.

Albert points to the underside of the bed. "Mattresses were held up with rope so they were off the floor and away from the bugs. When the mattresses would sag, they'd tighten the ropes, making the bed more comfortable. Hence the saying, *sleep tight, don't let the bedbugs bite.*"

"Well, if anyone would know about bedbugs, he would," Shay whispers.

Downstairs in the kitchen, the fireplace is big enough

to stand in. The lady tells us that girls didn't go to school as much as boys—that they typically stayed home to learn how to take care of the house. My mind bites into that and I can't stop thinking about it.

No more school.

Ever.

I lean over. "Albert, do you think that time travel is possible?"

He whispers, "Albert Einstein had extensive theories on its possibilities. And I certainly wouldn't argue with *him*."

"Me neither," I say to him. "How do you think I would look in one of those dresses and bonnets?"

He looks puzzled.

Finally, we go to a colonial schoolroom and join the rest of our class.

A lady talks about what a *visionary* Noah Webster was to create the first American spellers and dictionaries. Before that, people used to just make up spellings—there were no right or wrong ways to spell.

Some visionary. This spelling stuff is all *his* fault, since he's the one who got it in his head that we all needed to spell the same way.

I'm thinking Noah Webster was a scoundrel and they should have put him in jail for this.

The lady tells us it took him twenty years to write the

dictionary, and he also wrote the first schoolbooks and grammar books. I think he must have been tipped off his rocker, as my grandpa used to say.

"Students in colonial times didn't use paper and pencils like you do now." The lady holds up a little chalkboard in a wooden frame. "They used slates like these and wrote their answers down to show their teacher." She passes out slates, which are fun to write on. I draw a picture of Pierre with his beret and wish I had some green chalk to add a little smudge in honor of Albert.

The woman takes out a pointed white hat. "Now, this is something teachers began to use in schools toward the end of Noah Webster's life. It is called a dunce cap. As a punishment for misbehavior, a child would have to wear it and stand in the corner facing the wall."

I hear giggling. Shay is showing her slate to a bunch of other kids.

There's a head wearing a dunce hat and "Ally" is written underneath.

"What's the fuss about?" the guide asks as she walks over. Then she turns to them. "That isn't very nice. Erase that, please."

I stand, willing the tears that come to my eyes to stop. Knowing they will only give everyone more to make fun of.

"Are you all right?" the guide asks me.

Everyone is quiet now. They are all watching me. It's worse than the laughing. So I run out.

Out of the room and out of the museum. A woman calls to me, but I keep going. Out the door and around the back. Across the lawn of a beautiful light green house. I find a swing set, which reminds me of my grandpa, and how we spent hours on them at the park. I try to think about what he'd say now and am sad that it's hard for me to remember his voice exactly.

My hands slide down the chains as I sit on the seat, thinking of when I was little. When my world wasn't such a heavy place. I used to love to swing as high as I could—leaning back, reaching for a bright blue sky with my feet—and it made me feel like I could do anything. Reach anything.

I lean my cheek against the cool chain, feeling like I can't reach anything anymore. Then the tears come.

And then, standing in front of me, are feet. The shoes on them belong to Mr. Daniels.

He stands for a while without saying anything until he finally says my name. All I can do to respond is sniff.

"Can you tell me what happened in there?"

I don't know what to say. Such a small question and such a giant answer. "Please just leave me alone."

He takes a couple of steps away and stays quiet for a bit. Then he says, "My brother and I used to love to write in the sand on the beach. When my family would go to Maine."

I don't answer him.

Then he picks up a stick and writes something in the dirt under the swing next to me. More words. Why can't I ever get away from words?

He turns toward me and I stare at his knees. "Ally," he says, holding out the stick, "do you want to write something?"

I shake my head. I think of flying on swings through bright blue skies and away from words like *dumb* and *freak* and *loser*.

He squats down in front of me. "I'm sorry about whatever it was that upset you. Let me help."

I take a deep breath, and when I let it all out, the words come with it. "Nobody is ever going to be able to help me. Not ever. They all said I should have a dunce cap and they're right. That's the thing. They're right!"

"Oh my . . . Ally, you actually believe that, don't you?" I can hear that it's a shock to him.

I finally look up at him. "Why wouldn't I?"

"Because you are most certainly *not* dumb, Ally."

"You're just saying that."

"No, I'm not, actually. For one, you are amazing on

those bus driver math problems. You're one of the kids who gets the really harder ones correct."

I look up into his face with the bright sun behind him and blurt out, "But how come I can't read?" It's the first time I've ever asked the question out loud. I guess because I am so desperate for an answer.

"Aw, Ally," he says, "this thing that makes school hard for you . . . I think you might have something called dyslexia. And it means that, although it's hard for you to read, it doesn't mean you're dumb." He laughs a little. "In fact, you, Ally Nickerson, are far from it. Your brain just figures things out differently than other people."

I'm different; he's got that right. But no way am I smart like he says. "You don't understand."

"Yeah, Ally, I think I do." Then he leans in. "And you know what? You're brave."

I so want to be brave, but I'm not.

"Coming to school every day, knowing what you're in for. Knowing school will be hard. And that other kids are going to razz you. And you still come every day and decide that you're going to try again."

I stay quiet, just thinking about what he said. Hoping he knows what he's talking about.

"And you know something else? In some ways, you're a lot smarter than other kids. You can also do things they can't. For one, you're an amazing artist. Those drawings of yours! Wow, Ally. You've got talent there. What do you think about that?"

"I think it's like saying 'I'm sorry you're going to die but at least people are going to bring you flowers.'"

He laughs really hard now. "See that? Seriously, Ally. Only smart people say things like that." His voice drops. "It's going to be okay, kiddo."

I have never hoped for something so much as this.

"You and I are going to figure this out together. As a matter of fact, I already spoke to Mrs. Silver and Miss Kessler, the reading consultant at school. I was already planning to call your mom and talk to you tomorrow. We're going to give you some tests."

I deflate. "Oh, *no*. Please, no *tests*."

"Not the tests you're used to. You'll see. These are more like puzzles and games than tests, but the results will help us help you.'"

I feel like I can look up for the first time.

"You *are* smart, Ally. And you are going to *learn* to *read*."

A chill runs through my whole body. I don't have any choice but to believe him, because I can't go another day thinking things will be like this forever.

I wipe the tears from my face with the back of my hand. He stands up and we start walking back.

Mr. Daniels looks up at that bright blue sky and says,

"Now, don't be so hard on yourself, okay? You know, a wise person once said, 'Everyone is smart in different ways. But if you judge a fish on its ability to climb a tree, it will spend its whole life thinking that it's stupid.'"

I think hard about that. Could it be that simple?

A mind movie flickers in my brain of an angry fish at the bottom of a tree, banging on the trunk with its fins and complaining that it can't climb it.

I think of a turtle making a sandwich.

A snake playing the violin.

An elephant knitting.

Penguins playing basketball.

An eagle scuba diving.

But mostly I hope with every tiny bit of myself that Mr. Daniels is right about all of this.

CHAPTER 30

Miserable King

Two days later, a lady named Miss Kessler pulls me out of class early in the day to give me some tests. Mr. Daniels is right. They are more like puzzles and games than those awful bubble tests we do, where I just fill in circles without even reading the questions. She's really nice, like Mr. Daniels.

After school, Mr. Daniels is setting up a chessboard and pieces at the reading table.

I walk over and he looks up. "So, did your mom tell you that I called?"

"Yeah. She didn't say much, though. She usually has a lot to say about everything."

He laughs. "Moms usually do." He motions toward the chair. "Have a seat."

I pull out the chair, wondering what this is all about.

"Okay," he says, loosening his tie like we are going to do some serious work. "Chess is a game about planning. It isn't like other games where you just capture the powerful piece." He points to a piece with a cross on top. "This is the king. The object of the game is to trap your opponent's king, but not actually capture it. When you put your piece in a place where it could take the other king, it's called 'check.' When you give the other king absolutely nowhere to go, it's called 'checkmate.' And that's how you win."

Normally, I would be nervous and my mind would go blank, but he just has this relaxing way. His voice makes me calm. Maybe because I know he will never say anything mean. Call me lazy or dumb. And I know he wouldn't think it, either.

"Got that so far?"

I nod.

"So, then. Are you going to capture my king?"

I hesitate. Did I mess up already? "Didn't you say that you don't capture it? That you just make it miserable?"

He laughs. "Yes, I did say that. Good, Ally. Good listening."

So he goes through the rest of the pieces. The queen is the most powerful and can travel in a straight line in any direction. There are eight pawns that, when you band them together, can be strong. Most players take them for granted, though. He tells me that's a mistake.

The rooks look like castles and travel in forward, backward and side-to-side lines across the whole board. The bishops travel diagonally in straight lines, and the knights can jump in an L shape. The king can only move one spot in any direction. It stinks to be the one with the target on your back and be the one who can't go anywhere.

He has made up a sheet with pictures of the pieces and arrows to show how they move. He says it is in case I need a reminder. I turn it over, looking him square in the eye, and say, "I don't need that."

He smiles a little but never takes his eyes off of me as he reaches down and moves one of his pawns. "*Good,* then."

When I start to make some dumb moves, he asks, "Are you sure you want to do that?"

The first game ends fast, but on the second game, I capture his queen. The most powerful piece on the board. I stand up so fast, my knees push my chair back and it falls over. I want to ask if he let me do that, but I'm afraid of his answer.

He holds up his hand to high-five me. "Well done."

And it is so weird. I don't have trouble with this game. I like it. I like planning what I will do to trap his pieces. He shows me how you can work it so you put your piece in a place where it can choose between taking two different pieces; then your opponent has to choose which one to let go. That's called a "fork." I love the look on his face when I manage one of those and take his bishop. Like it hurts a little, but he likes it, too.

The longer we play, the better I can see it in my head. I can see what the board will look like a couple of moves from now. I learn to predict what he might do.

I see a mind movie where chess pieces come to life. They can travel around on the board all day by themselves and they are happy that they don't have to just stand there and wait for somebody to pick them up and move them. I know how relieved they are, being able to do something for themselves.

CHAPTER 31

Lots of Ways Home

"So, did your mom tell you that we talked?" Mr. Daniels asks.

"Yeah." I take a long breath, noticing that I can feel my own heart beating.

"I have to talk to you about something."

This doesn't sound good.

"I need your help."

"You need *my* help?"

"Yes, I do. You know how Miss Kessler gave you those tests?"

"Yeah."

"Well, it appears you do have dyslexia, which, like I said, makes learning to read difficult, but doesn't mean you're not bright. In fact," he says, half smiling like Travis, "you're very bright, Ally. The tests show that, too."

I shift in my seat.

"But you will need some help with learning to read better, and we're going to get it for you. Thing is, it might take a little time. Sometimes the paperwork and meetings around that take a while."

"Okay . . ."

"You know how I said we can't play chess on Tuesday or Thursday? Well, that's because I'm taking classes to get a degree in special education. Basically, it's a degree to help me help kids like you. Kids who are smart but have learning differences."

Smart? Learning differences?

"So I spoke with Mrs. Silver and Miss Kessler." He leans forward. "And your mom, of course. And we were thinking that I could help you after school a couple times a week. Until we can get you into formal services here at school."

I open my mouth, but he holds up his hands. "I know. Staying after school with me will be torture. But it would really help me out with the projects I have going on for my degree. You'd be doing me a huge favor. And I'd be so grateful, Ally." He leans forward. "So?"

I swallow hard. I'm not dumb. I know I'm not doing him a favor as a much as he's doing me one. And I can't believe or imagine what I've done to deserve help like this. Stay after school? I'd *sleep* at school if it would help.

I nod.

And we shake on it.

And he looks kind of dopey and happy.

I shift in my seat again. "But can I ask a question?"

"Sure!"

"What are 'learning differences'?"

"Oh! Okay . . ." He thinks. "When you ride your bike home, is there more than one way to go?"

"Yeah."

"I thought so," he says. "Well, just like there are different ways for you to get home, Ally, there are different ways for information to reach the brain. You have five senses, right? Taste, smell, sight, hearing, and touch."

I nod.

"So, what if an alien landed in a spaceship and you had to explain what the word *frozen* means without using the sense of touch? What if you had to use just words? I think that would be hard. Do you?"

"Yeah . . . it would."

"I think you've had some trouble learning words with just your eyes. We are going to incorporate more of your senses to practice letters and sounds. And I want you to relax about it. We'll have fun. I won't give homework on this. No tests to study for or anything like that, okay?"

I nod.

"Have you liked playing chess?"

I nod, hoping we can play today.

"You know, I had a feeling you would be good at it. I think your mind learns in pictures, and it helps you be a really good chess player. We've played several times now and you have learned it fast and improved a lot without much time. Also, thinking in pictures?" He leans forward. "It's one of the reasons you are such a good artist."

"Okay," I say, thinking this all sounds good so far. The only thing that worries me is that it won't work. I still won't be able to read.

"Good, then," he says. "We're going to practice writing letters. But we won't use paper and pencil." Then he pulls out a huge metal sheet and hands me a bottle of shaving cream. "We're going to use this, and by writing in shaving cream, you'll use sight and touch, and write large enough to use your whole arm. Just more ways for the signals to get delivered to your amazing brain."

I smile.

"Now, fill that giant sheet with foam and let's get started."

As I draw my finger through the gooey cream, I think about the words "learning differences." And I'm filled with fear and happiness and questions. But I'm mostly filled with hope.

CHAPTER 32

Screen Time

The day has been pretty good, and it just keeps coming. When I get outside, Mom and Travis are waiting for me in the car.

"We're going to head over to a friend's house to use their computer to Skype with your dad," my mom says. "We are all missing him so much, I thought it would be good."

The screen flickers at first, but then there he is. In his tan fatigues.

"Daddy!" I say, not able to hold it in and sounding like a little kid.

"Ally Bug! You're so big! How are you, sweetheart?"

"I'm good, Daddy. How are you?"

"I'm good but homesick. I sure miss you guys."

I think how there's a word for him missing home but not a word for us missing him.

He holds up some of my pictures. "I love the pictures you sent. I hang them up around my bunk. The other guys are jealous." He winks.

I can tell that Mom wants to cry, but she doesn't. She says that being a soldier's wife means being strong for him. She doesn't want him to know how hard it is without him here. He has enough to worry about over there. I sometimes wish she would tell him. I sometimes wonder if he would come home if he knew.

"Good, Daddy. I miss you. *So* much."

"I miss you, too, honey. You know I do. How are things? More silver dollar days or wooden nickels?"

"Some of each, I think. But more silver dollars lately. My teacher is cool. He is . . ." And I find I can't even explain it in words. "*Great.*"

"That's terrific, sweetheart!"

"And I have two friends, Keisha and Albert. Keisha likes to bake and she's brave. You'd like her, Daddy! And Albert is like a computer; he is so smart. He's a little nuts, though. He's been telling us how he loves all of the standardized testing. He actually thinks it's fun."

"Fun? *Testing?* He sounds like a different kind of guy."

"He is. And there's a girl named Shay at school who isn't very nice to me." I feel rushed, like I have to get everything in fast.

"Well, you'll always run into people like that. You can hold your own, I bet."

Mom pats me on the back. "Have to give Travis some time, honey."

"Okay." And I watch a movie of myself being strong and saying good-bye and not crying. But I want to be able to step through that screen and wrap my arms around my daddy. It feels like a part of us all is missing and we won't be whole again until he's home.

"*Hey*," Dad says. "Remember, Ally Bug, I *love* you. There isn't anything in the world I love more than you, your brother, and your mom."

I nod.

Travis sits down next.

"Hey, son! How are the big plans coming?"

"Not so great."

"What's going on?"

"Nothing," Travis says.

"C'mon. Maybe I can help."

Travis glances at Mom and me. "Well, this new manager came in at the garage. The old guy used to let me do my thing, you know. But this one hangs over me. Always asking me to follow the specs in the manuals. If I do something, he wants to know what page I looked it up on. I know how to work on different cars. I don't need to look it up."

My dad takes a long, slow breath. "Well, that does sound rough. Have you tried talking to the guy? Or having him talk to the old boss?"

"The old boss is out with back surgery for a while." Travis shakes his head. "This new guy . . . he just doesn't get me." His voice cracks.

My father leans forward, resting his elbows on his knees. Now he looks like he wants to crawl through the screen. "You'll get there. I know you will. And this is temporary. Just try to work hard and learn everything you can."

Travis nods but looks at the floor. I hear him mumble, "There are some things I just can't learn."

"I'm proud of you, Trav. You know that." He clears his throat. "I'm sorry I'm not there with you."

"Yeah." Travis looks up at the screen. "Love you, Dad."

"Love you, too, son. Hang in there. It will get better."

Travis nods, but I can tell he isn't buying it. Then he stands. "C'mon, squirt. Let's give Mom and Dad some time."

"Why?"

He pulls me over. "So they can talk mushy in private, that's why."

We sit down at the kitchen table and Mom's friend gives us sodas.

Travis cracks open his and takes a deep breath.

"*What?*"

"I'm just so frustrated, Al. There's so much I want to do, but . . ."

I want to help him. "Maybe we could head out to some junkyards like we used to and see if we can find something worth fixing up."

"Maybe. I'd love to find another old Coke machine or something in someone's barn. Buy it cheap and fix it up on my own." He looks at me. "You know I can turn almost anything around for some good money."

The words are the same, but they are heavy. There're no wiggling fingers or talk of being a genius. And my big brother looks so serious.

"I know you'll have Nickerson Restoration someday, Travis. And it will be part mine because of the name, right?"

He turns back and laughs, but it isn't real. He spends the rest of the time looking out the window, and I rack my brain trying to figure out what I can do.

Mom calls us back to say good-bye.

Dad puts his hand on the screen.

All three of us put our hands on the screen, too. Just as he flickers away, Mom leans over and leaves a lipstick kiss on the glass. Then she rests her forehead there and stays awhile.

CHAPTER 33

Possibilities

Working with Mr. Daniels gets easier because I am happy. But the work is really hard for me.

He has written *cat* on the board and we talk about the sounds. I can only hear one sound—cat—but he says that the word *cat* has three separate sounds. It feels like he's telling me the sky is yellow. As I say each of the sounds, he has me tap them out on my fingers. It does seem to help. It forces me to make them separately even though they are all one word. But it's a tiny word, and I worry what I'll do about whole books. Will I ever be able to do this?

When we are all done for the day, he leans back in his

chair like Travis would. "So, you are doing great, Ally. You really are. How are you feeling about all of this?"

"I'm actually happy to do this extra work, and I never thought I'd ever say something like *that*."

He smiles. "Good. I'm glad."

"But . . ."

"Yeah?"

"I guess I still wonder if I'll ever feel . . . if I'll ever be able to read the same as other kids and be . . . *normal* . . . and not to have to have all this extra help. It seems impossible."

He becomes serious. Then he takes out a piece of plain paper and pulls the cap off of a marker with his teeth. He begins to write.

IMPOSSIBLE

"Do you know what that says? Remember to break it into chunks. This is a long one, though, isn't it?"

I nod, trying to sound it out. "*Important?*"

"No, but that's a good try. It says *impossible*. Like you just said. You told me you think it seems impossible to read as well as everyone else."

"Yeah," I say, wondering why he had to write it down for me. It's not like I need a reminder.

Then he draws a red line between the *M* and the *P* and hands it to me.

IM/POSSIBLE

"I want you to rip the paper in two pieces. Right where that line is."

I do.

"So, now, Ally . . . that big piece of paper in your hand says *possible*. There is no *impossible* anymore, okay?"

I swallow and look down at it and I feel a little dizzy. The way he says it makes me feel like it could actually be true.

"Now, throw that little piece with the 'I-M' on it in the trash. It's gone forever."

I walk over to the garbage and drop it in. Watch it twist and spin as it falls. I look up and lock eyes with him and wish I had the words to tell him how grateful I am for his helping me. In this world of words, sometimes they just can't say everything.

"All right, then." He nods. "You head home. I have some homework to do or I'll lose my recess."

"Okay." I laugh, but I'm still thinking of the word on the paper. "Thanks," I say, looking down at it.

"My pleasure," he replies, and takes a folder out of his briefcase.

I stare at that word, "P-O-S-S-I-B-L-E," all the way down the hallway. I study the red color. I draw my fingers over the letters. I even smell the paper so I can take it in somehow.

I really want to believe.

CHAPTER 34

Birth of a Star

Keisha, Albert, and I walk to Albert's after school.
Keisha and I asked if we could come over and see his
house and he shrugged and said, "Okay."

The whole time, my hand is in my pocket, holding on
to that piece of paper. *Possible.*

Albert's house is big but dark and dusty when we enter. There are piles of things everywhere. Not papers like
our house. I mean piles of things with tubes and wires.
Things I don't recognize.

His mom greets us. "Hey, Albert! You have guests?"
Her tone tells me that this never happens.

"Yes, I do. These are my friends, Keisha Almond and
Ally Nickerson. Ally and Keisha, this is my mother,

Audrey Dubois," he says, waving at each of us, and she comes over and shakes our hands.

"Can I get you anything to eat?" she asks, sounding nervous.

Albert pauses. "No, thank you. We'll just go upstairs."

His mom says okay as we are already following him up a skinny, twisty staircase.

"What kind of host," Keisha begins, "doesn't allow his guests to have food? Dang it, Albert! I wouldn't have minded some!"

"It wouldn't be logical to offer you something that doesn't exist."

"But she offered it to us," Keisha says.

He opens his backpack and begins stacking his books on his desk like a pyramid. "I can assure you that the refrigerator is quite empty. In fact, it hasn't been plugged in for a week."

"Oh," Keisha says, her voice getting quiet. "I'm sorry, Albert. I really am."

Now I know why his mom's voice sounded funny when she offered, and why he eats so much at school. "Yeah, me too," I add.

He turns, surprised. "Why?"

Keisha scrunches up her face—the look she gets when she really can't figure him out.

"Well," I say, "because you don't have food. Or a

refrigerator. It must be terrible to be hungry and not be able to eat. And it's probably embarrassing for you. Maybe. I mean, I think it would be. I guess."

He tilts his head. "Filling the refrigerator does not fall within the parameters of my responsibilities. Therefore, the lack of food therein would have no reflection upon me whatsoever."

We are silenced. I don't know about Keisha, but I couldn't answer that for a million dollars. From the looks of her, I don't think she can, either.

I finally lift my gaze from his face to look around his room. Just a bed, a desk, and an empty trash can. The carpet and his blankets are all dark green. But his walls have colorful posters, all science-related. There is one I like the most. A picture of outer space, but with every color you can think of all swirled together with an orange glow off to the side. It's beautiful. I point at it. "Albert, what is *that*?"

"*That* is the birth of a star. The single most important thing that can happen in space. Well, the single most *positive* thing, anyway."

"It's beautiful!" I say.

He stares at it. "Indeed, it is," he says, sitting down at his desk.

Keisha laughs. "You're going to be a star one day, Albert. You'll do something amazing."

"I don't like . . ." He shifts in his seat. "I don't wish to be in the limelight."

"Limelight?" I ask.

"I don't like a lot of attention."

"Well, you better get used to it, Albert," Keisha says. "Because there is no way on God's green earth that you won't have boatloads of it when you go out and cure cancer or discover another planet or something."

"That's my hope. I want to change the world. Do something good."

And then, all of a sudden, I feel sad as Keisha goes on about how famous Albert will be. How he'll be written about in history books and stuff.

"Hey," Keisha says, poking me. "Why so serious over there?"

I'm thinking about the things Albert and Keisha will do and how I can't even read. I can't tell them that, though. So I try to sound happier. "I'm not that serious."

"Oh, yes, you are! *Dead* serious. You need to smile!"

"I *am* smiling," I say.

"Well, someone better tell your face about it."

I hesitate. "Can I tell you both a secret?" I ask, reaching into my pocket to touch my *possible* paper that I've carried since I got it.

"Yeah, of course."

"And you won't tell anyone?"

"Yes. Now, what's the secret we won't tell anyone because that's what the definition of *secret* is?"

Albert is quiet, but his head is tilted to the side.

"I . . . I have never really told anyone this, but . . . I have a lot of trouble in school. With reading and writing and . . . well, everything but math and art."

Keisha laughs. "That is *not* a secret!"

And then I feel terrible. And I feel my eyes beginning to sting. I start walking away, but she pulls my sleeve and pulls me back. Albert looks upset.

"No! That's *not* what I mean. I mean that we *know* that. But it doesn't *matter* to us."

"However," Albert says, "I do wish it was easier for you. We will not share your secret."

"Mr. Daniels says I have something called dyslexia, which makes it hard to read letters. That's why I've been staying after school, so he can help me."

Keisha is wide-eyed. "Extra school after school? That's terrible. I mean, terrible."

I want to tell her I'd spend the night at school hanging upside down in the closet if I could just *read*. "I don't mind. He's nice to help me."

"And we'll help you," Albert says.

"But I worry that maybe he can't help me," I say. And

then I mumble, "It . . . it makes me feel like I'll grow up to be a nobody."

"How can you *say* that?" Keisha asks.

"Well, you'll probably have some big successful baking company and Albert will . . . do whatever in the world Albert will do. And I'm just hoping to read a menu in a restaurant."

Keisha steps up and puts her arm around my shoulders. "You say he's going to help you, right?"

"You say"—Albert adds and then pauses to think—"that you'll grow up to be nobody. But logically . . . if *nobody*'s perfect . . . well then, you must be perfect."

"Perfect? Me? Uh . . . no," I say.

"You are pretty perfect, Ally," Keisha says, laughing. "Do like Mr. Daniels says. Be yourself. Be who you are."

"You know," Albert says, "I've wondered about that saying. And I can't ever find an answer anywhere on the Internet."

"What do you mean?" I ask.

"'Be yourself.' You always hear that."

"So?" Keisha asks.

"Well," Albert begins, "what if you don't know who you are?"

I get what he means, I think.

"People ask what you want to be when you grow up.

I know what kind of grown-up I want to be. But I don't know who I am now." Albert stretches his legs out. "There are always people ready to tell you who you are, like a nerd or a jerk or a wimp."

I think how it's hard not to believe the bad stuff.

"Look at it this way," Albert says. "If you had to be in a tank of water with a killer whale or a stonefish, which would you choose?"

"Well, duh. Who is going to choose a killer whale?"

"Well, in the wild, killer whales never attack people. Like never. A stonefish is way more dangerous with its thirteen venomous spines. It's the words. If the killer whale were called the friendly whale, no one would be scared."

And I think of words. The power they have. How they can be waved around like a wand—sometimes for good, like how Mr. Daniels uses them. How he makes kids like me and Oliver feel better about ourselves. And how words can also be used for bad. To hurt.

My grandpa used to say to be careful with eggs and words, because neither can ever be fixed. The older I get, the more I realize how smart my grandpa was.

CHAPTER 35

A Picture Is Worth a Gazillion Words

We have a sub. This is bad news.

Then it gets even worse. We begin with an assignment to write about a person that we know who is brave.

I start to come up with reasons to get out of the assignment. Go to the nurse? I haven't yet met a sub who says no to a trip to the nurse when you tell them you're going to throw up on their shoes.

I put on my "sick look." Just as I'm about to raise my hand, the sub turns to the class. "Where is Ally Nickerson?"

Huh? *Freaky.*

I raise my hand.

"Oh, I have a note here that says that you don't have to write, so you can just draw a picture of *your* person."

My face gets hot.

"Well, that figures," Shay says. "She can practice her coloring. And then there will be Play-Doh and nap time."

My toes curl in my sneakers and I slide down into my chair. The sub looks at Shay and shakes her head, but kids are already laughing, so what's the difference?

The sub gives everyone else a piece of lined paper and she gives me a plain one.

I sit, stunned. Wondering why Mr. Daniels would do this—betray me. Now I feel like I really am going to throw up.

I stand and have to concentrate on walking to move toward the door.

"Where are you going?" the sub asks.

"Out."

"You come back here and do your picture. *Now.* I mean it."

"I'm finished."

"What are you talking about? It's blank."

"No, it's not blank. I drew a ghost in a blizzard."

As the door slams behind me, I hear kids laughing at my answer.

Soon I am keeping Mrs. Silver's chair warm.

"So, Miss Nickerson. I must admit that I have enjoyed not seeing you lately. Things seem to be better with Mr. Daniels as your teacher. He's keeping you in line?"

"Yeah. He's a *peach*," I say with cut in my voice. "Are you going to call my mom?"

"No, I don't think so."

"I want you to call her. Please call her."

"Why?"

"Please?" I ask. I don't even know why I'm asking exactly.

She looks surprised but is silent. She dials the phone and talks for a bit. Tells her that I've had a tough day. Then she hands the phone to me. "She would like to speak with you."

I take the phone from her.

"*Ally.* What in the world is going on?"

I try not to cry, I really do, but the tears leak from my eyes. Everything is so tight inside and I'm so tired of it being this way. It's not like I wake up every day planning to be a failure. And I thought I had finally found someone to help me. And then Mr. Daniels pulls this . . .

"Ally? Did you hear me?"

"Mom?" is all I can get out, but it's squeaky and filled

with longing to pull her through the phone wires to sit with me.

I hear it in her voice. She feels as upset as I do. "Put Mrs. Silver back on the phone."

Mrs. Silver listens for a bit and finally says, "Oh. Okay, Mrs. Nickerson. We'll be in touch, then."

I head to the bathroom and sit in a stall long enough for the evidence of crying to go away.

When I get back to class, I ask Keisha to help me write a note so I'm sure it's all correct. I leave it on Mr. Daniels's desk: "I'm never reading after school or playing chess with you ever again. Not ever."

That afternoon, I drop onto my usual spot at Petersen's. I wonder what my mom will say about the call from school.

When she comes over, she kisses the top of my head. Which says it all.

"So, a ghost in a blizzard, huh?" She smiles at me.

I half smile. "Yeah."

"Pretty funny, I think." She leans over and puts her hand on my cheek, and it's everything I can do not to cry right there in front of everyone.

"I trusted him," I tell her. "He was the first teacher who . . ." And I stop because I can't say the words.

"You know, honey, I bet there's an explanation for

this. I bet Mr. Daniels didn't mean for this to happen. Give him a chance, okay?"

I nod. I hope she's right, because I want to think that Mr. Daniels doing something mean to anyone is like a fish swimming upside down and backward.

CHAPTER 36

In the Game of Life . . .

First thing, Mr. Daniels calls me into the hallway.
"So, I heard there was a little bit of trouble yesterday."

I fold my arms.

"Teachers often leave special instructions for a sub, but she was not supposed to share my notes with the class. I figured I'd write her a note telling her you could do a picture so she didn't pressure you to write . . . I know that you struggle and I thought I was helping you. But I see I shouldn't have handled it by singling you out that way. Ally, I think you know I would never hurt you on purpose."

I do know that. And I am so relieved to hear him say it.

"So, I'm sorry, Ally. I really am. I hope you can forgive me." He holds out his hand to shake. And I shake back.

That afternoon, Mr. Daniels moves his king, placing it on a black square between his own bishop and my knight. And I see the three of us. Albert, Keisha, and me.

With Keisha as a bishop. Tall and powerful and able to move across the entire board in one move.

With Albert being the king—the piece with a ton of value but the one unable to move more than one space at a time. Always taking tiny steps. Always running from and hiding behind the others.

And then there's the knight. The piece that Mr. Daniels says is the clever one. The best piece for catching opponents in a fork. A piece that moves only in an L. I feel like I am the knight, as I've spent my whole life jumping over things.

Shay is the queen. The piece with the most power to move and frighten. The piece most protected and sacrificed for.

I realize that dealing with Shay every day is like playing chess. She is always looking for your weakness, always trying to get you flustered and force you into a mistake. Against her, you have to remember that the board is always changing and moving. Keep your eyes open. Be careful. Have a plan. Realize that you can only stay on the defensive for so long—eventually, you have to take a stand. But no matter what, don't give up. Because, every once in a while, a pawn becomes a queen.

"Well?" Mr. Daniels asks, pulling me from my mind movie. "You've been thinking a long time over there. Thinking about your move?"

I look back down.

I search. I haven't beaten him lately and I so want to.

And then I see it.

It's the knight. The answer is in the knight.

I pick it up, move it, and hold my finger on the top to be sure I haven't made a mistake.

Yup, I've put his king in check and given him nowhere else to move.

"Checkmate."

He throws up his hands but seems happy.

"You didn't let me win, right?"

"Ally. I have three brothers. I am not *capable* of letting someone win." He laughs a little. "I think you're just invincible." And then he winks and begins taking the pieces off the board and putting them in the box. I am sad the game is over and I'm relieved that I trust him again.

And isn't it funny—I've gone from invisible to invincible.

CHAPTER 37

A Chicken, a Wolf, and a Problem

Because it's Fantastico Friday, Mr. Daniels has planned a puzzle for us to solve.

He draws some squiggly lines from top to bottom on the board and tells us it's a river. Then he proves he is the worst artist ever by drawing a chicken, a wolf, and a bag of grain on one side of the water.

"Mr. Daniels! Did you draw that with your eyes closed?" Oliver yells. "No offense, but that's terrible!"

He laughs. "I'm not offended, Oliver. I have eyes to see it." Then he looks at me. "We are not *all* wired to be gifted artists."

Then he adds a little boat, which looks a lot like a banana, on the bank of the river.

"Okay," he says. "Here is your problem to solve. You need to get all three of these items across the river, but you can only take one item at a time in the boat. You can't leave the wolf alone with the chicken because the chicken will become lunch. You can't leave the chicken with the grain or the grain will become lunch. So, how do you get all three items across the river? Remember, only one item in the boat at a time."

"Easy!" Oliver yells. "You just take the chicken first."

"What happens after that?"

"Then you take the grain."

"But what will happen to the grain when you go back for the wolf?"

After a couple of seconds, Oliver drapes himself over his desk. Mr. Daniels pats Oliver on the back. "It's okay, kiddo. It's supposed to be hard."

Mr. Daniels turns to Suki. "Any idea?"

She puts her pointer finger on her chin. "If you take grain first . . . wait . . . if you take wolf . . ." She sighs and shrugs. "I don't know."

Albert's eyebrows are so scrunched up, they look like they'll cover his eyes.

"Take a few minutes to try to solve this on your own. Then we'll talk about it in a bit."

I can't figure it out. No one can. Most kids have drawn a river and the animals like Mr. Daniels did. After a while, kids start talking to each other. I'm surprised when he doesn't tell us to be quiet while we try to keep solving it.

I tear off three little pieces of paper and draw the chicken on the first, the grain on the second, and the wolf on the third. I move them around, back and forth across the river. The class is loud now. I pick up my three pieces of paper and ask Mr. Daniels if I can work in the hallway because of the noise.

"Sure. Go ahead."

I'm out there just a few minutes, moving my pieces around, when Shay and Jessica come out. They sit across the hall from me. I guess they came out here to work, too?

"This is dumb," Jessica says.

"Tell me about it," Shay answers. "Who cares about chickens and wolves or whatever."

"Do you know the answer, Ally?" Jessica asks.

"Why are you asking her? Of course *she* doesn't know," Shay says. She whispers something to Jessica, and soon after, Shay is holding up signs with words. "Can you *read* this, Ally?"

I try to ignore them. I am not going to let her see me upset. I remember: Life with Shay is like playing chess. Don't get flustered. Don't make mistakes.

"Aw . . . you can't read it, *can* you?" The baby voice doesn't bother me as much as the words themselves. I try to concentrate on solving this problem.

Shay moves closer to me. "You. Are. *So*. Stupid, Ally. You know, Mr. Daniels is only nice to you because he feels sorry for you."

"C'mon, Shay? Let's go back inside," Jessica squeaks.

"Don't 'c'mon' me," Shay snaps. "Whose side are you on?"

"I'm on *yours*," Jessica says. But it isn't the sound of loyalty. It's the sound of fear.

I stand up, go into the classroom, and go into the corner behind Mr. Daniels's desk.

It's hard for me to push the sound of Shay's voice out of my head. But I remind myself that just because someone says it doesn't make it true. I concentrate on the three pieces of paper. The chicken, the wolf, and the grain.

I move the pieces of paper around on the floor. It takes me a while, but I realize that you need to take more than three trips. You need to take the chicken and then the grain, but then take the chicken back with you and leave it while you take the wolf. Then you leave the wolf with the grain and go back for the chicken.

I leap up. "I got it!" Keisha and Albert are surprised. So am I.

Mr. Daniels comes over and I whisper the answer in his ear. "Impressive work, Ally!"

He says I can go around and help others for the last remaining minutes. "Ally?" Max says in a loud whisper. "What's the answer? Come tell us how you did it."

By now, Shay and Jessica have come back in, and they see me helping Max. When I swing by her, Shay says in a low voice, "You're still a loser, Ally. A total and complete *loser.*"

But Jessica smiles a bit at me.

Mr. Daniels calls us back to our seats. "Okay. That was a two-part assignment. The first was to solve the puzzle. The second was to see who would stick with it. Who would work on it and work on it until it was solved. Congratulations to the few of you that did.

"If you are one of the many that gave up and started talking to your friends about soccer and other things, I want you to consider that no matter how smart you are, success is reached with hard work, too."

I can't believe it. My experience with endless frustration and having to work on things for so long has actually paid off.

I guess maybe "I'm having trouble" is not the same as "I can't."

CHAPTER 38

Loser for President

"So, Fantasticos," Mr. Daniels says, **"I've told** you about nominating a class president for our first ever school-wide student government. Do we have our first nomination?"

Jessica raises her hand. "I nominate Shay."

Shay looks back at her and turns forward. She looks like she's ready for her crown.

"Okay, good. Another nomination?"

No one.

"C'mon. We can't have an election with only one name."

I wait, glancing around. I know there will be no more names because Shay has made it known since Mr. Daniels first announced the election that anyone who runs against her will regret it. In fact, their children and their children's children will regret it. And she can actually do something like that.

Nope. There will be no more names.

Albert raises his hand. Whoa, Albert. Way to be brave. I glance back at Shay, whose eyes are now little slits.

But then Albert just asks to go to the bathroom.

After waiting and prodding, Mr. Daniels finally says, "I'll draw a name out of a hat or tell the council that we don't have a representative. C'mon, folks. Step up."

Another wait. Then Shay raises *her* hand.

"Well, Shay, this is good sportsmanship. Who will you nominate?"

She cracks a smile. "I nominate Al-ly Nick-er-son."

Wait. *No.* She didn't say me? I look back at her staring at me while Mr. Daniels compliments her again.

And then it hits me like a boulder. Of course. She wants to win, so she nominated me. A surefire loser.

"Is that okay?" Mr. Daniels asks me.

"Can I say no?"

"Yeah, you can say no, but I think you should run."

I really, really want to say no. Just not to him. "Okay. I'll do it . . . I guess."

"Good," he says. "Now, both of you will need to say a few words tomorrow, and the voting will follow."

"Oh, I get to write a speech!" Shay says to Jessica. Then I hear her whisper.

I am terrified. I can't write a speech.

After school, Mr. Daniels apologizes for not being able to help me today because he has class at the college. However, he suggests that I just be honest about why I want to be president of the class. He asks if my mom can work with me that night. I tell him that she will. I know she would in a heartbeat, but I would never ask her to help with this. It would just get her hopes up.

I figure I should write something down if Shay is going to. I'll look like a baby with no speech. So I sit down at our dining room table with a blank piece of paper—all bright white and staring at me and making my head hurt.

I want to ask my mom for help so bad, but if she knows I'm running for president of the class, she'll get excited. She'll want it even more than me.

I'm afraid to want it.

But a mind movie shows me at the front of the class and Mr. Daniels congratulating me, and I have to admit that I really would like it. I pick up the pencil and concentrate real hard. Real. Hard.

When I write, I press on the paper too hard, but I can't help it. It makes my hand hurt. I try to spell as best I can. It takes me an hour and a half to write two paragraphs.

I finally go to bed, praying for a high fever, the kind of sickness the whole town talks about. The kind of sickness that Albert would find super interesting. A good reason to not show up tomorrow.

CHAPTER 39

To-Shay

On the way to school, I wonder about taking the long way. Like through Mexico.

When I arrive, the first thing I see is Albert, who has a black eye.

"Albert," Keisha says, "when are you going to teach those boys a lesson?"

"It's nothing," he says all serious, and then gets happy. "Look!" He holds up a big sign for me.

**ALLY IS YOUR ALLY.
GIVE HER YOUR VOTE!**

"You made me a poster for the election?" I ask, smiling.

I know I'm going to lose, but this makes it okay. "Thank you, Albert."

He looks proud.

"But, um . . . Why does it say my name twice?"

"Your name is a homonym."

I should know better than to question Albert.

"You know, a word with the same spelling but different sounds and meanings. A-l-l-y spells your name, but it also spells 'ally' with a long 'i' sound at the end. An ally is someone who is on your side. Someone who sticks by you. Like allies in wars."

Shay comes by with Jessica. She looks at the poster. Then at the three of us. "Good luck, six-legged freak. I guess Ally will get *three* votes, anyway."

After they leave, I look at the three of us and think about how there are three primary colors. Yellow, blue, and red. Those three colors create every other color ever.

Keisha goes over to talk to Suki while I take a deep breath and turn to Albert. "I know I'm going to lose and Shay will never let me forget it." I look down at the desk and see Albert's sign. "But at least I'll have a poster." I smile at him. "Can I bring it home?"

"Yes, but you can't give up," Albert says.

"Okay. Well, maybe you're right, Albert. But you shouldn't give up, either."

"I am not nominated for class president."

I point at his black eye. "But you got beat up again, didn't you?"

He shifts his weight and looks away. "It's hardly the same," he says, and I feel sad that he doesn't see that it isn't too different.

Then Keisha returns. "Are you ready for today?"

"No." I shake my head. "Ready for public humiliation? How do I get into these things?"

She leans over and whispers, "You'll do a good job. Albert and I are voting for you no matter what you say in your speech."

I half smile. "What if I say you have to lick the lunch tables clean?"

"Well, I just won't do it. That will be easy," Keisha says, pushing my shoulder.

Albert adds, "It depends what we have for lunch that day."

We laugh. I'm happy that he doesn't seem mad about my questioning him.

Mr. Daniels is wearing a George Washington tie. He gets up and calls Shay to present first. I notice she is dressed in red, white, and blue. I look down. I didn't even think about wearing anything special.

Shay talks about how great she is and all that she'll

do. Kids applaud over her promises. Some of the things she says she'll do I can't imagine how she would pull off. Like extra recesses and longer snack times. When she promises new, bigger lockers for the hallways, I know she can't do that. With every sentence, kids are happier and I feel smaller and smaller.

I get up there, holding my paper. The sound that comes out of my mouth doesn't sound like a real word. I try again and get the same sound. Then four more times. The quiet laughs rise all around me, but Mr. Daniels holds his palm toward the class without taking his eyes off me, and the noise stops.

I feel hot. Then Etch A Sketch brain hits me and I go blank. Staring at a page.

That *I* wrote.

That I can't read.

Shay looks smug and it makes it even harder.

Mr. Daniels bends over, resting his hands on his knees. He whispers, "*Look*. You can *do* this. And you can hit it out of the *park*, too."

I shake my head a little.

"I . . . be*lieve* in you, Ally. Now, forget what you wrote. Put the paper down and take a deep breath. Close your eyes if it makes you nervous to see everyone and just be honest. Be . . . *you*."

He slides the paper out of my hands and I stand there silent for too long. I do close my eyes, wishing it would block their view of me as well.

Mr. Daniels's voice is gentle. Almost a whisper. "I want to be president of the class be*cause* . . ."

"I think it will be fun . . . and I think I would like it," I say, eyes still closed.

"*Good* . . . keep going," he says.

"I promise to be honest . . . I promise to work hard . . . I promise to listen to everyone who has ideas—not just my friends—because I would be in charge of the *whole* class. Well, not in charge exactly . . . but I want everyone to have a chance to give their ideas. I'll go to meetings and I would try to get extra things, like recesses, but I can't promise that I can do something like that." I open my eyes and look at Mr. Daniels. "*Can* I do that?"

"Actually, no. You don't want me fired, do you?"

I shake my head, feeling kind of dazed.

"Do you have anything else to say?"

"I don't think so?"

"Okay, then." He motions toward my seat and I sit down, stunned that it's over.

"Now for the vote!" he says.

He begins to pass out little pieces of paper.

"Wait!" Shay says. "All the other teachers have just had everyone raise their hands."

"Well, I thought it should be more like a real election. A secret ballot. Everyone will write the name of their choice for class president on the paper and fold it up. I will walk around to collect them."

"That's not fair!"

"Well . . ." He shrugs. "If it's good enough for the U.S. government, it's good enough for us."

I smooth out the tiny piece of paper and try hard to be neat.

There's a lump in my throat as I write down my own name, and I don't even know why.

Maybe because I'm not writing it down on a sign-in sheet for detention or signing an apology for something.

I fold it one, two, three times and put it in the basket when Mr. Daniels comes by.

He says he'll let us know later, but everyone begs him to count now. So, he does.

He opens the first one. "*Shay.*"

He opens another. "*Shay.*"

He opens a third. "*Shay.*"

But when he opens the next four, they are for me. And I'm surprised.

A couple more for Shay and then four more for me. Four more?

I can't imagine who would vote for me. I thought everyone loved Shay, but as I look around the room, some kids are glancing at me. And some actually look happy—Oliver and Suki and a bunch of other kids.

Toward the end of counting, when it looks like I've actually won, Shay crosses her arms and falls back against her chair.

In the end, Mr. Daniels shakes hands with Shay and tells her she ran a good campaign. Then, he turns to me and says, "Congratulations, Madam President Nickerson." And then he salutes me and laughs. The class claps. Keisha is up and dancing while Albert gives me a single nod.

"Mr. Daniels!" Max raises his hand. "I think this calls for a party!"

"Why, Max? Because it's Wednesday?"

"Any day is a good day for a party, Mr. D!" he says, and Shay looks annoyed with him.

But her real dagger eyes are saved for me. At least she's quiet for once.

And that's all perfectly fine with me.

CHAPTER 40

Tears of
Different Kinds

Keisha and Albert call me Madam President every chance they get. At the end of the day, we head out the front of the school and I am just. So. Happy. Like I could fly happy.

A loud, sharp voice interrupts my happiness. "What do you *mean*, you lost? You *lost?*"

Shay is standing with her mother.

"After all that time we spent writing that speech?" she says. "Did you *look* at the audience? Did you *speak* up? And smile?"

"I did. I did all of that. The other girl just got more votes."

Shay sounds like someone completely different. The

Shay I know, always so quick to pick a fight, now has a voice that sounds like a kindergartener. "Sorry, Mama." She brushes a tear from her cheek.

"Man," Keisha says. "That woman is *fierce.*"

"Geez, I can't believe it, but I feel sorry for Shay," I say.

"Uh-uh. No way," Keisha says. "Don't be feeling sorry for her. It's not an excuse to go around doing terrible things to other people."

"Yeah. I guess you're right."

"Have you learned nothing?" she asks. "Of *course* I'm right!" We laugh and she gets on her bus.

All of a sudden, I'm in a rush to get to A. C. Petersen's.

Running through the glass doors of Petersen's, I forget that I was going to be cool about telling my mom that I'm class president. I forget about telling her like it's any other thing. Instead, I jump up and down and say it loud enough that some of the regulars congratulate me before she does.

Her face says she's trying to figure out if she heard me right.

"Yes!" I say, nodding furiously. "Mom! They voted *me* class president. The kids in my class! Not the teacher. The *kids* did!"

She holds her arms out and I run into them. "I'm so proud of you," she says in a shaky voice.

I know why she's crying. I can't believe it, either.

CHAPTER 41

Not-So-Secret Letter

In that foggy time between sleeping and being awake, before I even open my eyes, I already remember that I am class president. I ask myself if it was a dream, knowing that it wasn't. Knowing by the way it feels like my insides are rising into the air even before I sit up. It's like when you wake up on Christmas morning and remember what day it is.

I lie there thinking that I'm happy Mr. Daniels counted the votes in front of everyone. I don't think I would have believed him if he'd just said I'd won later.

When I get to school, everyone acts the same, but I feel different. I put my stuff away and head to my desk, where I find an envelope with my name on the front. Weird.

I sit down and slide it off the desk. Glancing around, I pull a piece of paper from the envelope. I expect it will be a note from Mr. Daniels congratulating me. But it's not.

It's a full page of cursive writing. I recognize some of the words, like *love*, but I don't know what most of it says. The name at the bottom is Max. I look over at him and he nods once. I look away, feeling like my face must be glowing like Rudolph's nose.

I fold up the letter and slide it into my pocket, wishing I could read it. I think that when I get home and can study it, I may be able to figure it out. But I can't stare at it now. I look over at Keisha, who is putting her things in the closet.

"Hey," she says, sitting down.

"Hey." My mouth opens to tell her about the note, but she's not the best person at being quiet about things, and I'm afraid everyone will find out about it.

So I take a deep breath and decide it will have to wait. I don't have a choice. I'm both happy and mad at myself. Happy about the note and mad I can't read it. Max is cute and I like the red-and-white football jerseys that he wears all the time. And now that I think he likes me, I think I might like him, too.

"So how does it feel to be president?" Keisha smiles.

Oh yeah. Man, this may be the best week of my entire life. "Same old stuff," I say.

"Huh. Same old stuff? Already gone to your head?"

"Don't worry. I'll still talk to you and everything."

"Like you could ever ignore me." We both laugh.

"Okay, my Fantasticos!" Mr. Daniels begins. He reminds us to put our homework in the basket and gets the class helpers working on lunch counts and stuff. And I sit up straighter. Feeling like I have a place in this class.

After Mr. Daniels finishes with the boring morning stuff, he says, "One more thing. Our new class president, Ally Nickerson, has her first student government meeting today. So, if you have any suggestions for her, please let her know. If you have ideas for changes, she's the one in charge."

I know that I shouldn't smile, but keeping my mouth from smiling is like trying to keep Travis from loving cars.

The first suggestion I get is from Oliver. I'm trying to do my work and he stands in front of my desk. "I have a suggestion."

"Okay. What is it?"

"I think we should be able to bring candy for snacks. Like piles of it. Like dump trucks backing up to the school with the warning beeper going. And then it would dump, like, a huge pile of candy in front of the school and the kids could use shovels to collect it, because that rule they made this year about healthy snacks is dumb and took away the only thing about school I liked and—"

"Oliver?" Mr. Daniels interrupts.

He looks up.

"You have a question?"

"I'm giving my advice to the president. I have an idea."

He half smiles. "Okay, then. Well, finish up and get back to your seat."

Oliver looks back at me. "Okay? Can you do that?"

"I'll try?"

He looks disappointed.

Suki interrupts. "I disagree. The healthier snack rule was good. It is bad for your body to fill with candy."

He looks over at her. "Stop acting like you're a grown-up. Geez."

Other kids give me suggestions, too.

Just before lunch, I hear Shay complaining that if she'd been elected, she'd have started a horseback riding club at school. For a second, I feel bad, and then I realize she couldn't possibly do that. Horses? Where would we get horses?

I think about starting a Fly to the Moon Every Thursday club. And a mind movie plays in my head of a silver rocket with blue stripes flying to the moon with Keisha, Albert, and me strapped in. Albert calmly explains the energy required to lift the rocket. Keisha is screaming, she's so happy, and I'm laughing because I'm happy they're happy.

I'm pulled out of my movie by Shay, who's standing in front of me. "Everyone agrees. You should go crawl into a hole and never come out."

"Since I won the election, I guess not everyone feels that way."

And I'm surprised that instead of saying something back to me, she just stomps off.

At the end of the day, as we are getting ready to board the buses, Shay tromps up to me with her shadow, Jessica, right behind her. "So, did you get the letter?"

Why is *she* asking me about that?

A little voice in my head warns me. "What letter?"

Shay glances behind her and turns back. "You know. The *letter*."

"What are you talking about?" I ask.

She is impatient. "The letter . . ." She drops her voice to a whisper. "From Max saying you should meet him for lunch. You never showed. He is really disappointed."

Oh. "He is?"

She glances behind herself again. "So, do you like him?"

"Why did he want to see me at lunch?"

"Ally. You can't just ignore something like that. It's *rude* . . ."

I see Max coming but don't say anything.

She continues. "He really likes you, so you should answer Max's letter. And say the thing in it that he says to. Okay? Will you tomorrow?"

"What letter?" he asks.

"Max? Oh, hi," Shay says, stumbling over her words.

"What letter? You said my name."

I never thought I'd see Shay unable to talk.

"Actually," I say, "the love letter Shay says you wrote to me." I hand it to him. "Thanks very much, but I'm busy."

"Um . . . wait. I never . . . I didn't actually . . . ," he says to me, trying to be nice. Then he looks at the letter and at Shay and Jessica. And he doesn't look so nice.

Jessica turns pale. But not as pale as Shay does.

Whatever was going to happen at the lunch table is something I'm lucky to have missed. It's the first time ever I've been grateful not to be able to read.

CHAPTER 42

The Gifts of No Excuses, Scotch Tape, and Antibiotics

Mr. Daniels calls me up to his desk. *"Here.* I have something for you."

I'm excited. Until I see it's a book. Not like I hate them like I used to. But they still scare me.

I stare at it. Hoping he just wants to book talk it. Not actually read it.

"I'd like you to read this."

I open my mouth to speak, my mind already rolling out multiple excuses.

He puts his hand up. "Listen, Ally. I know it won't be easy. I know it will take time. But the thing is . . ."

My excuses become harder to say.

"I think you can read this one. And I want you to try."

I reach out and take the book, which has a picture of a kid holding a goldfish bowl.

I flip through the pages. The book isn't long, as far as chapter books go. That's a relief.

I look up at him and hold his gaze. Normally, I'd be giving him all kinds of reasons I can't do this. But the thing is, Mr. Daniels could hand me a book as heavy as a boulder and I'd try to read it.

Just because he asked me to.

"Okay, we are going to begin a unit on persuasive writing," Mr. Daniels says. "So I'd like you to tell me, if you could have an unlimited amount of any single object, what would it be? It can't be magical, have special powers, or anything like that. Just an ordinary, everyday type of object."

"Well, obviously"—Shay speaks slowly, like she's talking to a little kid—"wouldn't everyone just choose money?"

Albert looks confused. Not something I see too often. "The first thing I thought of was antibiotics."

"Really?" Mr. Daniels steps forward, putting his hands in his pockets.

"There are many who can't afford medications, so I would like to give them out to people who need them.

All over the world." Then he seems to be thinking out loud. "I wonder if antibiotics would help or hurt alien life-forms?"

"Well," Shay sputters, "if you had an unlimited amount of money, you could buy the medicine, right?" I catch her rolling her eyes at Jessica.

He shrugs. "I'd rather just have the medicine."

"Scotch tape!" Oliver yells. "I'd want Scotch tape!"

Most of us laugh along with him. "And why is that, Oliver?" Mr. Daniels asks.

"Because it's awesome, that's why. People don't think how tough life would be without Scotch tape."

Mr. Daniels nods. "You may have a point there, Oliver!"

"Or Elmer's glue. I love Elmer's glue. If I had barrels of it stored up in the garage, I could cover my hands with it every day. And then peel it off. I love doing that. And it grosses out my mom. I tell her it's skin."

Shay makes a noise.

"What?" Oliver asks her.

"That's ridiculous," she says.

"What's ridiculous?" he asks.

"The opinions of others are to be respected," Mr. Daniels says, but Shay and Oliver talk right over him.

"Wanting tape and glue," Shay says.

"No it isn't, because I would also use them with paper

to make notes for my little sister. They make her feel better."

"Make her feel better?" Mr. Daniels seems concerned. "Is she ill?"

"Oh, not anymore. But she had something that was called . . . well . . . it was long. It had five syllables and she had to go to the hospital a lot to sleep over. And when she'd go, I'd visit her and bring cards. And they made her happy. My mom says I was the one who helped her get better."

"I see. Well, Oliver, you get huge creativity points today." Mr. Daniels musses his hair. "You're one of a kind, you know that, Oliver?"

Suki raises her hand. "Grandfather says everyone is unique. Special. Unlike all others. That makes us each great."

"I like that, Suki!" Mr. Daniels says. "And *you* are indeed great!"

She remains seated but bows a bit. "*Thank* you, sir."

Mr. Daniels bows back and then stands up straight. "In fact, you're all great, my fantastic Fantasticos!"

Albert raises his hand and Mr. Daniels nods toward him. "Excuse me, but just because something is unique, that doesn't mean it's good. After all, E. coli, a dangerous bacteria, is unlike all others."

"Point taken, Albert, but I do like that people are all

different. What if we all looked the same, thought the same, had the same beliefs?"

"That sounds boring," Keisha says.

"Indeed it does," he says.

I think that I wouldn't mind being more like everyone else. But then I think . . . I wouldn't want to draw like everyone else. And I wouldn't want to act like Shay. Or Jessica.

All of a sudden, there is screaming. It is Oliver. "Ant murderer! Ant murderer!"

"What is it, Oliver?" Mr. Daniels asks.

He points at Shay. "Ant murderer!"

"All I did was step on a dumb ant. What is he so freaked out about?"

"You had no right to kill him. He was just walking by."

"You think it was a *him*? It's just a dumb ant. Who cares?"

"*I* care," Oliver says, getting down on all fours with a tissue to check on the ant, which is clearly dead. He cleans it up with a tissue and slips it into his pocket.

"You're going to keep it?" she sputters.

"Well, I'm not going to just throw him in the garbage. I'll bury him at home."

She begins to laugh.

"Shay," Mr. Daniels says. "There will be none of that."

She stops.

"We are all different. You care about some things and Oliver cares about others. We have to work to accept each other. Even though we may not agree."

"Yeah!" Oliver yells.

"And Oliver," Mr. Daniels says, "I think you have to cut Shay a break here. It's pretty common for people to step on ants."

"*So?*"

"Oliver?" he asks, and waits.

Oliver turns to Shay and mumbles, "Sorry." And climbs back into his seat.

"Thank you, Oliver." Mr. Daniels wanders over to Oliver's desk. "I'm glad you apologized. Now that you have"—he leans over and rests his hands on his knees—"I'd like to add that you have one of the kindest hearts I know. You care so much about everything. Always looking out for others. And that, my fine young fellow, is going to make for a great man someday."

CHAPTER 43

Set the World on Fire

After the teasing that Albert has taken for his shirt, Keisha and I decide to do something for him. The teasing hasn't seemed to bother him that much, but it bothers us.

So we made our own shirts to go with his.

We walk up behind him while he is organizing his papers into piles. "Albert, do you like our shirts?" I ask.

He turns around and stares. At me, with a shirt that says *Steel*, and Keisha, with a shirt that says *Magnesium*.

I think it's the first time I've ever seen Albert truly confused.

"Okay," Keisha says. "Get it? They match your shirt. But not the genius guy alone on the rock in space with his robots thing, because I told you I thought that was a bit creepy . . ."

Albert is still confused, so I interrupt. "The shirts match because the three of us together are going to set the world on fire. Like Mr. Daniels says."

"Yes," he says, "flint, steel, and magnesium are commonly used together for fire starters. I get it."

The corner of Albert's mouth twitches, which is like someone else doing cartwheels down the hall.

Without thinking, I yell to Shay across the room, "Hey! You tease one of us, you tease all of us!"

Shay has an expression like she's just smelled rotten meat and it makes Keisha and me laugh really hard.

Then I pat Albert on the back. "Just wanted you to know that you can always count on us."

"Well, that would make you either a set of fingers or an abacus."

"Uh, Albert. *Seriously?*" Keisha shakes her head and then leans forward. "It means we think you're a cool dude."

"We're *allies.*" I smile.

He goes back to arranging his papers.

"Yes, I know," he says softly. "I am most grateful."

CHAPTER 44

Tales of a Sixth Grade Something

Travis drives me to school because the project I did for our book report is too hard to take on the bus. I've always used my art for projects at school, but this is a three-dimensional scene on a piece of wood. A scene from *Tales of a Fourth Grade Nothing*. The book that Mr. Daniels gave me to read.

"What's gotten into you?" Travis asks. "Since when do you smile like that on a Monday morning?"

I'm going to school feeling proud for once. So I just sit there continuing to smile.

"Hey," he says, hitting me on the side of the leg. "I'm

happy to see you so happy about school, Al." He laughs a bit. "To be honest, I wouldn't mind feeling some of that."

When I get to class, lots of kids surround me. I guess it's because the project is so big.

Shay is the first to come over. She looks at the kitchen scene I have made mostly of paper, including a working light over the sink that Travis helped me make.

"How did you do that?" Shay asks, pointing at the lit light over the sink.

"There's a battery underneath."

She looks disgusted. "And *you* made that?"

Oliver comes over and grabs for the light. "Cool!" Before I can move, he knocks the wire, which makes the light go off.

Shay begins, "Oliver, you're such a—"

"Leave him alone," I interrupt. "If I don't care, you shouldn't."

Shay and Oliver are both wide-eyed but for different reasons. Oliver smiles a little.

"It's okay, Oliver. I'll fix it."

Shay is squinty-eyed for a bit and then laughs in a way that is louder than normal. She's pointing at my project. "I read that book like . . . four years ago. And there aren't any soldiers in it," she says, pointing at a picture hanging on the wall of the room I made.

Max comes over. "What's up?"

"She has a picture in here that has nothing to do with the book. Book report, Ally? Should be about the book?"

"Well," I say, feeling a little warm all of a sudden, "most houses have art on the walls, so I figured I'd decorate the room and drew a picture of my dad in his uniform."

"Wait!" Max brightens. "Your dad is in the army?"

"Yeah."

"That's cool. What does he do?"

"He's a captain with a tank division."

"Your father drives tanks? *Seriously?* That's awesome!"

I look up. "Thanks."

He holds up his fist to fist-bump me. And as he walks away, he tells the other guys about my dad.

From the look on Shay's face, she can tell that her insult backfired on her.

Then Mr. Daniels comes over. He's wearing a tie with books on it. "Wow, Ally! That is amazing!" He leans forward and drops his voice. "I am really proud of you."

My response is stuck in my throat. I watch a series of movies in my head, trying to see a time when a teacher has said this to me. There isn't one.

"Ally?" he says.

Still, I can't speak. Usually when I find myself unable to speak, it's because I'm humiliated. I like this feeling a lot more.

CHAPTER 45

My Brother's Question

I'm working on pictures of cupcakes that talk for an ad campaign for Keisha's business. She asked me to help her. It feels great to have someone ask me for help.

As I draw, I think about my sketchbook and how I love it but don't draw in it as much anymore. It used to be the only thing that made me happy. Now I have other things, too.

I hear Travis chewing gum in the doorway before I see him. Without looking up, I say, "Mom told you to stop chewing gum like a goat. The whole room is not supposed to hear you."

He goes silent. Weird.

I finish erasing a line and look over at him. He looks kind of stiff. Hands stuffed in his pockets. Then he takes one hand out and brushes his chin with his fist.

"Travis? What's wrong?"

"I just wanted to ask you a question."

"You want to borrow money or something?"

He does that half smile of his and shakes his head. But I can see the seriousness.

"You can ask me anything you want, Travis. What is it?"

He comes over and sits on the side of the bed. "That teacher of yours. Mr. Daniels. What does he do after school with you?"

"You mean chess?"

He shakes his head. "No. The reading. What does he do? I mean, do you just sound out words and stuff?"

I put down my pencil. "Well, we talk about words, but it's not the same as other teachers. Like we never use paper. Ever. He has me write letters in blue or pink sand. Or sometimes in shaving cream."

"Really? So you can read now?"

"Well, not yet. But it's getting easier. It can be like running up the side of a building sometimes. I get so tired. But I am doing better."

"So it helps? What he does?"

"Yeah. It's more fun than learning the old way.

Sometimes it's boring because he'll do a list of words that have some of the same letters in them. Like *light* and *might* and *night*. He writes the letters that repeat in every word in red and the rest in black. Then he makes the words into pictures so I can remember them better."

I flip my paper over. "Here. I'll show you." And I write *sun* with all these little lines around it pointing outward to look like the sun.

"And that really helps you remember it?"

"Yeah, and he also has these sheets of plastic that I can see through but are different colors. He puts those over pages and it makes the headaches better. It's like turning the brightness down on a computer. It's weird."

"No more headaches from reading? *Really?*"

"Well, I still get them, but they're not nearly as bad. Like a little stick hitting my head compared to a baseball bat."

Travis smiles and then stands up. "Well . . . I'm glad he's helping you. And I'm glad that you have Keisha and Albert, squirt. You're doing great."

"You're doing great, too, Travis! Not long before you'll open up Nickerson Restoration, right?"

He nods once and turns to leave. He doesn't talk about the neon sign he'll have or the big rolling tool cases or anything. I miss hearing his mouth running like a motor about all his plans.

"Travis?"

He turns. "Yeah?"

"*I* could try to help you?"

"Naw," he says, brushing his chin with his knuckles. "I don't need you to do that. I was just wondering."

CHAPTER 46

Flying Tigers and Baby Elephants

"Well, Ally," Albert says to me at lunchtime. "Before I really knew you, I used to call you 'the Flying Tiger.'"

"Oooh, Albert! That's a great name," Keisha says. "Like fierce. Like nobody messes with her, right?"

I wish that described me, but it doesn't. Why in the world would he nickname me that? I thought that Albert paid more attention to things. I look up and he is watching me.

"Well," he asks, "aren't you wondering why I called you that?"

I shrug.

"It's not an insult. Just my observation."

I shrug again. "Fine. Tell me, then."

"Before the United States entered World War Two, there were a bunch of American pilots in China. They were called the Flying Tigers. They flew those planes with the shark teeth on the nose."

"Wait!" I say. "My dad and brother love those planes!"

He nods once as I try hard to shake out the mind movie of me as an airplane.

"They did not have many planes, so they would repaint them every few missions. Change a bit of the design and the numbers so that the Japanese would think there were far more of them than there really were."

I sort of know what he means.

"I've watched you. Trying to figure out how to repaint yourself for other people all the time. Trying to make them think one thing about you when the opposite was true. Like with the teachers. Always getting sent to the office."

Wow. I can't believe Albert noticed all this.

"Okay," Keisha asks. "Do you name everyone like that?"

"I like analogies. They interest me and help me understand."

"What about me? Did you have a nickname for me?"

He hesitates.

"Okay, Professor. Spill it," Keisha says.

He bites his lip.

"Listen. You better tell me and tell me now."

"The Baby."

"*What?* The *Baby?* Are you *kid*ding me? She gets a great name like the Flying Tiger and you called me *the Baby?* What the heck is that supposed to mean?"

He turns red. "I didn't want to offend you."

"Well, it's just a little too late for that. I'm going to send you into space. Where no man has gone before. No kidding."

Is Keisha quoting *Star Trek* now? The girl has lost her mind!

"I called you the Baby because when you're quiet, you're taking everything in. But when you want something, you're loud about it and usually get your way pretty fast."

I burst out laughing. "Oh, man, Keisha. That is just too perfect."

She folds her arms with a bit of a "humpf" but then begins to laugh, too.

"Albert, do you have one for yourself?" I ask.

When he doesn't say no, I know it means yes.

"Tell us!" Keisha says.

"I'm the Elephant."

"Because you're big?" I ask.

"No," Keisha says. "Because he has a good memory."

"Elephants do have good memories," he says. "But that isn't why I chose it as my symbolic name."

"Then why?" I ask.

"Well . . . I've become a pachyderm."

"Is that a religion?" I ask.

His face twitches a bit. "No. An elephant is a pachyderm. It means an animal with a thick skin."

I guess we're all pachyderms, then. Or we pretend to be.

His finger picks at the side of his thumb. "Elephants feel a wide range of emotions, but their behavior remains constant. On the outside, happy and sad often look the same."

I can't remember the last time I had nothing to say about something. All this time, I thought that Albert was the science guy with as much feeling as a pinecone. But I was wrong. All that watching he does. All that thinking. He really does understand things. He definitely gets me.

CHAPTER 47

Great Minds Don't Think Alike

Mr. Daniels looks really happy as he makes an announcement to us one morning. "Today, my Fantasticos, we are going to jump from our social studies unit and talk a little bit about some famous people. People I bet some of you know."

He takes out pictures and stands them up on the tray of the board. They almost cover the length of it, and I worry that we will have a test or have to write about our favorite.

Mr. Daniels seems electric. "I'll say the name and then you tell me if you know why they're famous, deal? No need to raise your hands. Just call out."

Wow. He's breaking the biggest teacher rule ever.

He points to the first picture. "Thomas Edison."

Wait. I know who that is. I squeak out, "He invented the lightbulb?"

"Great, Ally. But if you know, don't answer like a question. *Declare* your answer!"

I imagine myself at a podium in front of thousands of people, arms in the air, declaring my answer.

"What about this one?" he asks.

Max says, "Alexander Graham Bell, who invented the telephone. I did a report on him."

"Most excellent work," Mr. Daniels says.

The next one is George Washington. Everyone knows that one.

"Henry Ford?" he asks.

"He invented the car!" I declare.

"Well, he did begin Ford Motor Company, but he didn't invent the car. He perfected the moving assembly line, which was a very clever way to build a lot of cars fast."

"Oh."

"Ally, how do you know about these inventors?"

"My mom bought a DVD called *Schoolhouse Rock*. It has a cartoon about inventors."

"Ah, yes. *Schoolhouse Rock* is awesome. Next one? Albert Einstein!" He says this one like he's introducing someone on a game show.

Albert raises his hand.

"Yes, Albert?"

"Albert Einstein was born in Germany on March 14, 1879. He is considered the greatest human mind to ever have lived in the fields of physics, mathematics, and philosophy. He changed all of science with his ideas. My father says that the field of science was like Pinocchio as the puppet, and Einstein changed it into a real boy."

"Does he really?" Mr. Daniels laughs. "That's brilliant. Is your father a scientist, Albert?"

"Yes, sir. He named me after Albert Einstein, so I know a lot about him."

Keisha whispers to him, "Is that why you style your hair after him?" She turns to me. "That boy has never even seen a comb."

"Style my hair?" Albert asks, confused.

Mr. Daniels walks back toward the pictures. "I have a feeling that Albert's father is quite a scientist indeed."

We go through the rest of the pictures.

Leonardo da Vinci, famous painter of the *Mona Lisa*. Also a gifted inventor.

Pablo Picasso, another famous painter, who created a modern style that no one had ever seen before.

Patricia Polacco, talented illustrator and author.

Whoopi Goldberg, hilarious comedian and actress.

Henry Winkler, famous actor and author.

Muhammad Ali, world heavyweight champion in boxing.

John F. Kennedy, thirty-fifth president of the United States.

Winston Churchill, prime minister of England during World War Two. His intelligence and grit kept the Nazis from taking over England. In fact, all of these people had grit to spare.

Grit. I like that word.

John Lennon of the Beatles.

Walt Disney, creator of Mickey Mouse.

Then Mr. Daniels stands back. "Don't you all agree that this is a stunning group of talent? Is there anyone here that would be willing to stand up and say that any of these people were stupid?"

Everyone shakes their heads.

"Albert gave us a great rundown of Albert Einstein. But did you know that he was kicked out of school when he was young? His report card said that he was too slow to amount to anything. He couldn't memorize the months of the year. In fact, he had trouble tying his shoes. But . . . he was and remains one of *the* greatest minds we've ever seen."

I remember when I had a hard time tying my shoes. Travis sat with me for a long time teaching me the baby way where you make the rabbit ears.

I stare at Einstein's picture with his crazy white hair that looks like he had an accident with a light socket. How could he figure out something like time travel and not know the months of the calendar?

Mr. Daniels says, "Some people say that John Lennon is one of the most gifted, spiritual musicians ever."

He walks over and points to Walt Disney. "What about this guy? Did you know he was told by a teacher that he wasn't creative enough?" He moves over. "How about Henry Ford? He was born understanding how an engine should work. He just *knew* without studying it."

Hey, that's like Travis.

He walks toward the windows. "Knew exactly how it should go together. He never went to school for it, but he was such a genius with machines, he worked as Thomas Edison's engineer for a while. He built his first car by hand by building a motor and putting it in between two bicycles. And with his idea of using a moving assembly line, he ushered in a new world."

He walks back toward the board.

"You know what all of these people have in common?" he asks the class. Then he stands in front of my desk and looks me dead in the eye. "Many believe that they all had dyslexia."

I feel it in my gut. In fact, I feel it everywhere.

He smiles a bit. "That's right. As children, they

struggled to read even simple words and, based on some other clues as well, most experts now believe that they had dyslexia. But, of course, we know their struggles weren't because they were stupid. It's just that their minds worked differently. And thank goodness they did, because otherwise we may not have telephones or light-bulbs or stunning works of art." He smiles. "Oh. And we wouldn't have Mickey Mouse."

He is quiet for a while. I think he's letting it sink in.

"So, then . . . for your homework, I have an extra-credit assignment." He turns on the smart board and there's writing:

Ju jt nvdi ibsefs up sfbe xifo zpv epou ibwf uif dpef.

The class is already complaining that they can't read it. Complaining that it makes no sense.

"It's a code," he says. "Each letter stands for another— extra credit for anyone who can crack it. It isn't exactly like reading with dyslexia, but it will give you a taste of how hard it is. How long it takes." Then he looks at me. "And how *smart* you have to be to persevere."

He dismisses us and everyone starts to get ready to go home. But I'm still staring at the pictures of all those famous people and wondering if they felt like me when they were young. Did they feel stupid? Did they wonder what would become of them?

Mr. Daniels squats next to me. "Ally?"

Although the room is loud, it's like the sounds are far away.

"Are you okay, Ally?" Mr. Daniels asks.

I turn to him and have to clear my throat before speaking. "It's true? All those people there . . ." I look back at their pictures. "All of those people couldn't read, like me?"

"Indeed," he says, smiling. "Not that they couldn't read. They just needed to learn a different way, that's all."

He puts an oval-shaped piece of metal in front of me. "This is a paperweight," he says. "It's a gift for you."

"For me?"

"Yes. Look." He points at each word as he reads them. *"Never, never, never quit. Winston Churchill."*

I pick it up. It's heavy.

"I'm not giving it to you as a reminder, because I know that you will keep at it. I've really gotten a sense lately of how hard you've had to work to learn what you have. And," he says, laughing, "you've fooled a lot of smart people. So, how smart does that make *you*?"

I swallow hard.

"I'm giving it to you because I want you to know that

I've noticed. And that you're going to be okay, Ally." He leans forward a bit. "*Better* than okay, actually."

My head swims with all that's changed.

In school.

And in me.

CHAPTER 48

Oliver's Idea of Lucky

"So, what's it like?" Oliver asks before his body has even come to a stop in front of my desk. "What's it *like?* This thing you have. Dystopia or whatever."

"Dyslexia?"

"Yeah. What's it *like?*"

"Well . . . ," I begin, but don't have an answer.

"Don't you see everything backward? That's what I hear." He squints. "Wait. Do you see me backward right now?"

I shake my head. "No. I don't think so." Then, a mind movie of the butterflies at the museum drops into my head and I look back up at him. "It's kind of like the letters on the page flutter like butterflies."

His face scrunches up. "Wait. You mean they move? The letters *move?*"

I nod.

His eyes widen. "That is *so. Cool!* You're so lucky. Letters just stand there all boring when I read. I hate reading. I'd rather do anything in the world than read."

"Really?" I ask, wishing that the letters would just stand still for me and wait to be read.

He gasps a little, as if he can't believe that I don't agree. "Uh, yeah? Are you kidding? Last summer, my mother kept giving me the choice of reading or washing her car. She had the cleanest car in the neighborhood all summer long."

I smile because I really like Oliver. I've been thinking about myself so much, I never really noticed how funny he is.

And looking around the room, I remember thinking that my reading differences were like dragging a concrete block around every day, and how I felt sorry for myself. Now I realize that *everyone* has their own blocks to drag around. And they all feel heavy.

I think of that word Mr. Daniels used when he talked about the famous people with dyslexia. *Grit.* He said it's being willing to fail but try again—pushing through and sticking with something even if it's hard. He also told us that a lot of those famous people were not afraid to make mistakes no matter how many they made. I think messing up will bother me less than it used to.

Keisha, Albert, and I are hanging out on the playground when Shay and a few of her clones come over. "So, you really have that thing that Mr. Daniels was talking about, right?" Shay asks.

"Yeah," I say, feeling proud of it after his talk.

"So, dyslexia . . . Don't you see letters backward or something?"

"Sort of," I reply, not sure exactly, since I've never seen letters the way other people have.

"Figures," she says. "My brother is in kindergarten and he can see them the right way." She looks at me like she always has. It bugs me, but not like it used to.

Albert steps forward. "Do *you* ever see letters backward, Shay?"

"No. Are you *kidding* me?"

"Oh," Albert says, dropping his voice. "Too bad."

"Why is that too bad?"

"Oh, well, you know it's a sign of intelligence." And then this thing just comes over Albert. Like he's all relaxed and everything. Standing in a way that isn't all stiff and Albert-like. "I know that you think I'm a nerd and everything," he says to her. "I mean, you've called me all kinds of things. But there is one thing you've never called me."

"What could *that* be?"

"Dumb. You've never called me dumb."

She swings her hip to the side and sighs. "What is your *point*, Albert?"

"Well, there are a lot of letters that I've always seen backward. And Ally sees more than I do. So, who knows how smart *she* must be."

Wait. Albert sees letters *back*ward?

Shay is thinking about it, looking like she just found out that she's the only one not invited to a party. "What letters do *you* see backward?"

"Well, O, I, T, A, M, V, X, U . . . and some others."

Huh?

Wow. Shay at a loss for words? I never thought I'd see that. "C'mon," she finally says. "I have better things to do."

"I'm going to the bathroom," Jessica says. "I'll be there in a second."

"*Obviously*," Shay says. "You wouldn't dare *not* be."

Shay leaves and her group follows. But they don't all stomp away like they usually do. A few walk behind her. Half looking back.

Jessica turns and jogs back to us, and I can tell right

away she's different. "Hey, I think it's cool. The dyslexia. And you really are a good artist," she says, and then turns to walk away again. Then stops. Turns back. "And . . . I'm really sorry, Ally. For everything," she says before turning to run this time.

My mom was right. "I'm sorry" are powerful words.

"So, Mr. Science," Keisha says, turning toward Albert. "Did the world just fall off its axis or what? Did I just see what I think I did?"

We all watch Jessica run up the hill.

"Well," he says, "there *is* an explanation. Ally is a catalyst."

Not sure what that means, but from Albert it must be good.

All of a sudden, Keisha starts cracking up. Bending over with her hands resting on her knees. Stumbling around like she's going to fall over. "God, Albert. I can't believe you did that with the letters. And I can't believe she went for it."

Albert cracks a smile.

Keisha puts her arm around my shoulder. "Albert here just gave Shay a whole bunch of letters that are the same forward and backward. If she wasn't spitting-nails mad, trying to hurt people, she probably would've figured it out."

Then I laugh, too. "Thanks, Albert," I say. "Shay is going to hate you more than she hates me soon."

"No worries," Keisha says. "That girl has plenty of hate to go around."

And I realize that it is easier now that Shay and everyone else know why I have so much trouble. Mr. Daniels says I should concentrate on what I do well. I'm going to try to do that.

When I get back to my desk, there is a wooden *A* on it.

I pick it up and wonder where it came from.

"Ally, my grandfather would like you," says Suki. "I carved this letter from one of his blocks. It is for you. 'A' for Ally. But also, I think you are amazing. And I admire you. I wanted you to know that."

I swallow the lump in my throat. "Thanks a lot, Suki. Now I can tell everyone I finally got an 'A' at school." And we both laugh.

I hear Shay across the room, but she doesn't sound happy.

There's something on her desk, too.

A pile of old friendship bracelets.

CHAPTER 49

I See the Light

During break time, Albert and Keisha are talking about her new ideas for recipes.

Jessica and Max and some other kids are laughing about something while Shay sits at her desk watching them. She seems like she's not sure what to do, which is an odd thing to see. Finally, she stands and walks over. However, they don't really acknowledge her. Especially Jessica. Something about it reminds me of those empty sundae dishes back when Shay and Jessica made me feel small for being me. Now it's hard to imagine feeling that way.

Oliver is going from desk to desk. As he does, kids are

holding their arms over their heads to make a big circle. Then he says something and they answer. When they do, he jumps and laughs.

Finally, he gets to Shay and I can hear what he's saying. "Hold your arms up over your head to make a circle."

She hesitates but does it, which surprises me.

"Now," Oliver says, "spell 'image,' and then say 'lightbulb.'"

"I-M-A-G-E lightbulb."

Oliver jumps and laughs.

Shay drops her arms. "You're such a freak, Oliver. Go stink somewhere else."

He goes to Keisha and they do the same thing with the arms, but she laughs afterward.

And I feel happy for Oliver because I remember a time when he would have sat down and been sad after Shay had said something like that.

Looking at Shay, I can tell she's looking around the room wondering where she fits in now. Wondering how all of this happened. I remember how it felt to be alone in a room full of people, so I take a deep breath and head over.

"Hey, Shay." Now that I'm close to her, I can really see how upset she is.

"What do *you* want?"

"Um . . . I just thought I'd say hi."

While she stares at me, all of the mean things she's done wind through my head and I wonder if I've made a mistake in coming over.

"I think," she says, "we should call you Alley Cat from now on. Go bother someone else."

At first I'm surprised, but then I realize it wasn't a mistake to come over, because it felt like the right thing. Shay's the one who decided to act mean, but at least I tried. I have to admit, though, I do feel sorry for her.

CHAPTER 50

A Hero's Job

Keisha, Albert, and I take our time walking home.

A voice behind us calls, "Hey, brain! Wait up!"

We turn around and I hear Albert mumble, "Oh no." I've never actually seen anyone turn white before, but he does. I look back at these three boys who are all running toward us. Albert is jumpy like he's going to run, too, and I know that they must be the kids that beat on him all the time.

I wish Travis were here.

"Who are *they?*" Keisha asks.

Albert swallows hard.

"Hey, brain," the one closest says. "Are these your *girl*-friends?" he asks.

The group laughs. One in back says, "Yeah, right. Like that dweeb would have a girlfriend. He'd be lucky to get a pet bird." They laugh harder.

Keisha steps forward. "Why don't you just get lost?"

"Don't think so. I'm right where I'm supposed to be." He turns to Albert and shoves him. "Hey, brain! Did you miss me?"

"Like a dog misses a flea," Albert mumbles, his eyes glued to the ground. I wish he'd at least look at the kid.

Keisha's voice gets louder. "Yeah, like a little flea. Now get lost before someone slaps you!"

And before I can even start worrying for her, the boy grabs her arm and pushes her on the ground. "Slaps me? I don't think so!"

"Hey!" Albert says. "You leave her alone."

The boy turns to Albert. "Shut up, brain. Or you're next."

The second boy picks up Keisha's bag. "What do you have here?" He turns it upside down, dumping everything out.

"Look!" the third says. "A book with sweet little cupcakes."

"No!" Keisha yells. "Give me my book back!"

Albert is shaking. Actually shaking.

"Hey!" I say. "You leave us alone!" And when the kid turns and looks into my eyes, I'm really scared. Like I'm going to throw up.

Keisha tries to get up and the first boy pushes her back down. He moves his foot to step on her but doesn't get the chance.

Albert—peace-loving, I-will-never-stoop-to-their-level Albert—pulls the boy away from Keisha. He turns him around and holds him by the front of his coat. The boy's toes barely touch the ground. "You do *not* touch her again," Albert says with a voice I didn't think he had.

Keisha jumps up and runs over to me. She stands next to me, squeezing my arm. Hard.

"I'm tired of you beating on me all the time," Albert says. "You have no right to treat me like that. And you don't even fight one-on-one. You gang up on people like cowards." Albert throws him down on the ground. Tosses him like he doesn't weigh anything. The two other boys charge, but Albert grabs one and throws him on top of the first kid. Boy three runs.

The first boy stands up. "You want to fight, brain? I'll fight you." He charges Albert and hits Albert in the stomach.

I've never seen Albert mad before. He hits the kid one time and the kid goes down. Through his moans, he tells his friend to get up and fight—to get Albert for him. The second boy sits up, like he's thinking about it.

Albert's feet are far apart, and he leans forward. "Do you *really* think you want to do that?"

The boy shakes his head.

Albert takes a step toward both boys on the ground. "Don't you ever touch my friends again. Ever. Or you'll answer to me."

Keisha and I gather her stuff and put it back in her bag. "C'mon," Albert says, looking at us before turning to walk away. We follow him.

I'm surprised that Keisha is quiet for as long as she is. I feel like I'm going to cry. Thinking how Albert has come to school every day with those bruises for all this time. We always asked him what it would take for him to fight back. Turns out it was protecting us.

"Albert," Keisha says. "That was *amazing*. And you can *fight*!"

"I can't take credit for strong arms."

"But," I say, "it wasn't just your arms, Albert. You were seriously *brave* back there."

"Yup. That's true," Keisha says. Then she laughs. "So, Albert, what got into you, anyway?"

"My dad has always said that violence is something to avoid at all costs," Albert tells us. "But he has also said that you never hit a girl. And so I had to weigh the two. I just . . ."

Then he stops walking and he's wide-eyed looking at me. It gives me a chill the way he does it. "But really," he says, "it just made everything hurt inside to watch them hurt you two, and I would have done anything in the universe to stop it."

When we arrive at A. C. Petersen's, Keisha is still acting out what Albert had done. He never says anything, but he seems quietly happier. And a bit taller.

After sliding into the booth, I take out my social studies book.

"Seriously? You're going to do homework after that?" Keisha asks.

"I have a lot to do."

"I thought Mr. Daniels said you only had to do half of the questions."

"He did. But I want to try to do them all. I don't want to get off easy." I've figured out that if I look at the first two letters and the last two letters of a word, I can sometimes figure it out from the rest of the sentence. This trick I've discovered made Mr. Daniels say I'm a genius.

"What is wrong with you? Are you serious?" Keisha asks.

"Yeah, I know. First I don't want to do work and now I want to do extra."

"You are a mystery, that's for sure," she says.

"Huh," Albert says. "That reminds me of our president Teddy Roosevelt, who went on a hunting trip and found that one of his companions tied a bear to a tree for him so it would be easy to shoot. He refused to shoot the bear and set it free. In fact, that's why teddy bears are called Teddy. After that president and that day."

Keisha shakes her head. "Man, you've got a story for everything, Albert."

"I do not provide the stories. History does."

"You know, Albert, you kind of talk like those guys who narrate the movies at school. From the History Channel and stuff."

"Why, thank you, Keisha."

Based on Keisha's expression, I'm not sure it was a compliment, exactly.

I lean forward and look at Albert. "You know what else is a tremendous achievement?"

"What?"

"Sticking up for friends against guys that have used you as a punching bag for months. You whaled on them, didn't you, Albert? You should get a medal or something."

Albert sits a bit straighter. "Well, it was just one thing I did on one day." He turns to me. "Not like you, Ally."

Huh?

"When Mr. Daniels told us about people with dyslexia . . . I mean some of the greatest minds the human race has ever seen . . . I've been kind of wishing I could have it, too."

Did he really just say that?

Keisha laughs. "Sometimes, Albert, I've thought you have nothing but facts stacked up in that head of yours. And then you do what you did today and say something like that. You know what *you* are?"

His eyebrows jump.

Keisha leans forward. "You are one good friend, Albert."

CHAPTER 51

C-O-U-R-A-GEnius

I ask Mr. Daniels if I can renew my book at the library, and he smiles like I gave him a cake. "Sure," he says. Then he hands me an envelope. "Since you're heading that way, will you give this to Mrs. Silver for me?"

"Sure."

"You have to hand it to her, though. And you have to wait until she opens it and writes a response, and then return it to me. Okay?"

I nod, thinking back to the days when a visit to the office meant trouble.

I renew my book and then head to the office. Mrs. Silver is there when I walk in. She smiles. "Hey there, Ally."

I hold out the envelope even before I start talking. I guess I want her to know right away that I'm not in trouble. "I have a message from Mr. Daniels."

She holds up a finger, telling me to wait one minute while she speaks with her daughter, and picks up the phone.

I mean to listen in on their conversation, but something else catches my attention. The poster with the two hands reaching for each other. The one I was asked to read but couldn't.

I walk over and stand in front of it. I stare at the outstretched fingers. Then I take a deep breath and look at the letters. I step right up to the wall and, just like Mr. Daniels taught me, use the envelope in my hand as a marker under the first line.

I whisper, "S-s-some . . . things?"

Mrs. Silver comes and stands behind me. She puts her hands on my shoulders. I stop reading.

"No, Ally. Keep going."

I turn my head to look up at her. "Can you just read it to me so I can hear it all at once?"

Mrs. Silver reads,

**"SOMETIMES THE BRAVEST THING
YOU CAN DO IS ASK FOR HELP."
—C. CONNORS**

"Ally?" she asks. I turn.

Her voice cracks. "I want you to know how sorry I am about the bumpy road we had for a while. I'm proud of all the strides you're making. All the hard work you're doing. We should have picked up on your learning differences before, but you were so bright . . . and, well, I hope you'll give me another chance to help."

I nod, looking over at that poster, and think how I should have asked for help. But, at the time, it took more bravery than I had, I guess.

"Hey!" she says. "Didn't you have a letter for me?"

"Yeah. Mr. Daniels said you are supposed to read it before I leave."

She opens the envelope and reads as she walks to her desk. Then she laughs and turns toward me. "Did he tell you what this says?"

I shake my head.

"It says, 'The student delivering this note is our student of the month for hard work and a good attitude.'"

"*Me?*" I ask. "Are you sure it isn't a mistake?"

She laughs.

"My brother, Travis, will *never* believe this!" I tell her. But in my heart I know he will. He'll be happy for me and mess up my hair and say, "Good going, Al!"

She writes a note for Mr. Daniels and hands it to me.

I leave the office and am told right away to stop

running by a teacher. So I do. But it is so hard not to run and jump and yell.

Mr. Daniels smiles at me as soon as I turn the corner into the room and I half jump, half run over to his desk.

"So, you got the message?" he asks.

I nod.

With a hand on my shoulder he says, "Attention, Fantasticos! I would like to announce that our student of the month is our own Ally Nickerson!"

Oliver slaps his desk while others applaud. Even Jessica. Shay says something I can't hear exactly, but I do hear Jessica answer her, "Stop it, Shay."

Albert and Keisha come over. Albert with a high five and Keisha with a hug. "Wow! Are you going to talk to us little people when you win your next award?"

"If you bake for me," I joke.

"Wait," Albert says. "Will you bake for me if I win something?"

Keisha and I laugh while Albert says, "No. I'm serious."

Keisha pats him on the shoulder. "Yes, Albert. I'll bake something for you."

We begin collecting our things to go home. Travis is picking me up because I have to bring my project home. I get my stuff and head down to the gym to wait.

Soon, Travis walks in, still wearing his clothes from the garage.

The sun from outside is behind him like he's walking out of a ball of light, and all of a sudden, I feel like I'm going to cry.

It makes sense. Everything does.

Travis is smart. In the same ways that I am.

I run up to him, put my project down on the floor, and throw my arms around him.

"Pretty happy to avoid the school bus, huh?" He laughs.

"I'm just really happy to see you, that's all." And I hug him one more time. But tighter.

His face questions me.

"Wait a second," I say. "I'll be right back!" And I turn and run before he can answer. I run because I just have to. This can't wait until tomorrow.

I sprint down the hallway, ignoring someone far behind me telling me to slow down.

I approach my classroom, grab the door frame, and swing into the room, out of breath.

Mr. Daniels looks up from his work, surprised.

"Ally?"

I step up to the side of his desk. I reach into my pocket and pull out the worn piece of paper that says *possible*.

"You're still carrying that?" he asks, and smiles big.

"Please, Mr. Daniels," I tell him. "You have to help. I'll do anything."

He stands. "What's wrong, Ally?"

"*Please* help my brother." I take a step forward. "He needs to learn to read, too."

I think of the poster in Mrs. Silver's office. Mr. Daniels's hand reaching for mine. And mine reaching for Travis.

"Of course, Ally. I'm happy to help. Your brother is picking you up today, right?"

I nod. Feeling so grateful for Mr. Daniels. I wonder if he knows that I came into sixth grade wondering what would ever become of me. Now I have dreams I know I'll chase down.

I'll set the world on fire someday.

And come back here . . . and tell him so.

"Okay," he says. "You go ahead. I'll be down in a minute to talk with him about what we can do."

I run from the room but slow down. Thinking. Aware of every step. Eventually I'm back at the gym. Back to my big brother, who has stood by me and helped me always. Who's believed in me no matter what I said.

Travis is standing there with his hands in his pockets, looking up at the light streaming through the windows across the top of the gym. I watch him for a while. Finally, he sees me and smiles.

I hand him the tattered piece of paper that says *possible*. "*Here*. This belongs to you now."

He looks confused. "For *me*?"

Mr. Daniels isn't far behind me. He shakes Travis's

hand. "Hello there, Travis. I've heard a lot about you." He looks down at me. "Quite a little sister you have here."

Travis does that half smile. "Yeah. She is."

"So," Mr. Daniels says. "Apparently, Ally thinks we should talk."

"Okay," he says, brushing his chin with his knuckles.

Mr. Daniels explains to him what we do after school and invites him to join us.

I look up. Travis swallows hard and nods. I knew Travis would be brave enough to say yes.

A mind movie lights up in my head. Of our last name written in neon lights in the window of Travis's new place.

And there's another mind movie. Of me being happy. Reading and making my art and finding a special Ally-shaped place in the world.

But these mind movies won't go into my Sketchbook of Impossible Things, because I know they will actually happen.

I lean my back against my big brother and feel his hands on my shoulders. Their voices seem to fade as I look up at that light streaming through the windows.

Things are going to be different.

It's like birds can swim and fish can fly.

Impossible to *possible.*

ACKNOWLEDGMENTS

The author would like to thank:

Nancy Paulsen, friend and editor extraordinaire. You are the 1943 penny of editors—one of a kind. And I am most grateful.

Erin Murphy. You are spectacular. I'm blessed that you are my agent and friend.

The Gango, who have added rich layers to my life—you are cherished.

The "Other Penguins" who have worked on the editing and design of this book: Ryan Thomann for designing the unique interior, Kristin Logsdon for designing this phenomenal cover, and Sara LaFleur, who is always there to happily lend a hand.

Carol Boehm Hunt, Jean Boehm, Karen Blass, Rick Mullaly, Jill Mullaly, John Mullaly, Melody Fisher, Bonnie Blass, David Blass, Suzannah Blass, Michael Mullaly, Megan Mullaly, Christopher Mullaly, Emma Mullaly, Dot Steeves, Margaret Pomeroy, Pat and Frank Smith, and ALL of the rest of the Smiths! LOVE this big family!

Extra thanks for my brother, Ricky, who helped me know and love Travis.

Extra thanks for my niece, Emma, whose beauty, spunk, and smarts helped me create Keisha.

Rere, who is with me each day on this astounding journey. I wouldn't have these blessings if you hadn't been my mum. *SWAK*

Mary Pierce, Liz Goulet Dubois, Laurie Smith Murphy—cherished friends, phenomenal women, and forever-time critique group partners.

Lucia Zimmitti, Jenny Bagdigian, Jennifer Thermes, Cameron Rosenblum, Julie Kingsley, Leslie Connor, Sarah Albee, Carlyn Beccia, Bette Anne Reith, Jeanne Zulick, Sally Riley, Linda Crotta Brennan, and Sharon Potthoff. You are each a treasure and have been an important piece of my journey.

Jill Dailey, Paula Wilson, Nancy Tandon, Jessica Loupos, Holly Howley, Kristina O'Leary, and Michele Manning, my new writing friends. Thanks for your keen eyes.

Susan Reid Rheaume, Kathy Martin Benzi, Kelly Henderschedt and Doreen Johnson. I'm grateful for you girls.

Peter Steeves, my cuz, who shared his early coin-collecting adventures.

Dr. Kevin Miller, USN, Yoshiko Kato, Marlo Garnsworthy, and Leah Tanaka, for your help with Japanese culture and language.

My Maine chess experts: Lance Belounqie, Gabriel Borland, William Burtt, Carther S. Theogene, Owen Wall, Matthew Fishbein, and Arthur Tang.

The following teachers and their 2012–2013 classes for being early listeners and helping to title some chapters: Ms. Melanie Swider, Mrs. Susan Dee, Ms. Pattie Uccello, Ms. Rachel Wulsin, and Ms. Wendy Fournier.

Audrey Dubois, Suzannah Blass, Molly Citarell, Abbey Citarell, Grace Bremner, Samantha Eileen Miller, and Chrissy Miller, who helped with some of the details. Thanks!

Susan Dee, Angela Jones, and Sharon Truex, early teacher-readers. I appreciate your time, wisdom, and support. Thank goodness there are teachers like each of you in the world.

Maureen Brousseau and Mary Begley, who taught me the most important things about teaching while at Gilead Hill School in Hebron, Connecticut.

Judy Miller, who taught me the most important things about myself.

Ms. Carol Masonis, Ms. Patricia Yosha, Ms. Anita Riggio, and Mr. Constantine Christy. Gifted teachers who were the best I ever had as a student. Life-changers, every one of you.

Greg—thank you for being you. Love always.

Finally, I could write volumes on how grateful I am for

Greg, Kimberly, and Kyle. Your creative gifts, intelligence, humor, and thoughtfulness helped to inspire these characters, and your love and daily support make the whole ride worthwhile. You've each given me more silver dollar days than I could have ever imagined. Love you all infinity times around Pluto. Again.

Dear Readers,

Like so many other adults, I started out as a kid.

I was typical in a lot of ways. Being a girl whose companions were often her older brothers or a neighborhood full of boys, I became good at climbing trees, skateboarding, and baseball. On a skateboard or holding a bat at the plate at the bottom of the ninth, I was confident. I felt like I could handle—and even excel at—what I was doing.

But sitting at a school desk was often a different experience. I remember sitting back and scanning the other kids in the class, wondering why I couldn't be more like them. How were they able to do their work so quickly? By the time I was Ally Nickerson's age, I remember sitting at our dining room table, staring at my brother's high school textbooks and wondering how I would ever get through. Like Ally, I wondered what would become of me.

Then, as a sixth-grader, I was placed in class with Mr. Christy, who would later serve as my model for Mr. Daniels. Little did I know he would change the path of my life. Why? Because he changed my perception—how I viewed myself—and that was so powerful.

My perception was that the other kids were just *better*. I learned later that they weren't—being better at taking tests didn't make them better; it just made them better test takers. But at first, I let those negative thoughts seep in. I began to assume that I wouldn't be good at things, so I went through a time when I didn't try as hard as I could. I just figured it didn't matter.

However, Mr. Christy had confidence in me. He had me tutor younger kids. He handpicked books for me to read and helped me move out of the lowest reading group. He smiled when I walked into the room. After a while, I began to mirror his confidence in me and left his class ready to set the world on fire.

We all have both our special talents and areas where we need to work a bit harder. Honestly, I've learned much more from—and have been ultimately successful because of—my failures. Things will not always be easy; sometimes we do fail. But it isn't failing that makes you a failure. It's staying down that does. The ability to stand up, brush yourself off, and try again is a *huge* strength. It's something that will take you very far in your life. Very far indeed. If you develop a habit of standing up and trying again, just *imagine* the phenomenal things that could be in store for you.

Thank you for picking up *Fish in a Tree*. I do hope you have enjoyed meeting Ally, Keisha, Albert, Mr. Daniels and the others.

And remember: Great minds don't think alike.

Take care,
Lynda